Perfection, thought Claire, the food, the wine, the setting

And the ruggedly handsome man sitting opposite her. This was the sort of magic moment she had yearned for back home.

"You said you travel a lot," she said. "You're not married?"

"Heavens, no!" Jake gave an edgy laugh, as if the idea seemed ridiculous to him.

That laugh annoyed her. "But haven't you ever—haven't you ever fallen in love?"

It was a silly question, she thought as soon as she'd asked it. But he just raised his brow a fraction and said, "Falling in love is a loser's game, Claire. Lust, yes. But I learned early on that the ones who travel fastest, are the ones who travel alone."

"That's an awfully cold philosophy," Claire said.

"Maybe I'm a cold man."

SALLY COOK lives in Norwich with her two small sons. She was a professional writer for nine years before she branched into romance fiction.

Books by Sally Cook

HARLEQUIN PRESENTS
1223—DEEP HARBOUR
1287—BELONGING

SALLY COOK

hijacked heart

𝓗arlequin 𝓑ooks

TORONTO • NEW YORK • LONDON
AMSTERDAM • PARIS • SYDNEY • HAMBURG
STOCKHOLM • ATHENS • TOKYO • MILAN

Harlequin Presents first edition December 1990
ISBN 0-373-11320-X

Original hardcover edition published in 1989
by Mills & Boon Limited

CHAPTER ONE

THE corridor seemed endless. Cream walls, red patterned carpet, and door after door after door, all identical except for the different number-plate screwed on to each one.

Claire Middleditch walked down the middle of the carpet. She looked at the doors. It would need to be a room near the far end, she thought: that was the sea end. A room on the left-hand side, with a balcony. No problem, that: all the rooms had balconies. But which one?

834, 835, 836...oh, what difference did it make? Come on, Claire, she told herself. Stop being such a craven coward, and get on with it.

She stopped walking, took a deep breath, raised her hand and knocked on a door. Room 839. She waited. Nobody opened the door. Perhaps she had knocked too gently? She tightened her fist and knocked again, rapping hard with her knuckles.

Still no response. Perhaps the room was empty. Try the next one. No, that had a 'Do Not Disturb' notice hanging outside. How about the next?

She knocked on room 841; no response. She waited a moment and knocked again, as hard as she could this time. No response. Another empty room? Surely not. She glanced at her watch. It was eleven-thirty in the morning: too late for people to be still in bed, too early for them to be at lunch. A good time. It should be: she had chosen it carefully.

5

But nobody opened the door of room 841, or room 842, or room 843. Claire had left this assignment to her last day as it was, out of her reluctance to go asking. Now it was essential that she get into one of these rooms. She bashed again, annoyed and increasingly worried, at the next identical wooden door.

Ow! Her knuckles connected with the sharp metal edge of the number-plate, and a little sharp pain ran through her hand and down her arm. She dropped her hand, and grabbed at it with the other one. She did a little war dance on the carpet, sucking at her sore hand to try to drive the pain away.

'If you've lost your key,' a lazy male voice said from somewhere behind her, 'there's always a reception desk downstairs.'

Claire spun around, fist still to her mouth, to see where the voice had come from. The door to room 839 was open now. And a man was leaning against the jamb, hands in the pockets of the tattered denim shorts that were his only garment, watching her make a thorough fool of herself.

'Oh,' she gulped. She had a strong urge to up and run, but he was between her and the lift, and there was only the blunt end of the corridor behind her. And this was—wasn't it?—what she had been trying for. She took another deep breath, and stepped a pace closer to him.

'I did knock,' she said, 'but you didn't answer.'

'On my door?'

'On your door,' Claire agreed.

The man looked her up and down. It was a slow process, not least because Claire was a tall girl. He took in her strappy flat-soled sandals, her baggy cream slacks, her green T-shirt, her light brown hair pulled back into a ponytail.

'No, don't tell me,' he said, in that lazy, mocking voice, which held a hint of a northern accent, 'do let me guess. The Mormons? No, they always wear suits. Jehovah's Witnesses? Wrong part of the world. The Moonies? Wrong colour, they're orange, aren't they? The tax inspector? The sanitation department? The police?'

'I'm a photo-journalist,' Claire snapped.

He could have told that for himself: the camera bag slung over her shoulder was unmistakable. He could have looked relieved, or even mildly impressed, like some men she had spoken to, or curious. In fact, he barely reacted at all. The only muscles that moved were those that brought about a barely perceptible narrowing of his languid stare.

'Then you picked on the wrong door, lady. The mass murderer's in room 739. One floor down.'

'That's nice,' Claire retorted. Just her luck! she thought ruefully. Only one door opened, and it let out the most exasperating man she could ever recall coming across. She wasn't going to get any joy from him, that was obvious. Perhaps she should go and knock on the seventh floor, after all.

She hitched up the strap of her camera bag, turned away from him, and began to stride towards the lift.

'You going to make me die from the suspense?' the man drawled.

Claire spun back round towards him.

'See the bag?' she snapped. 'It holds my camera. I'm a photo-journalist, right? And somewhere in this cursed hotel there's a really nice person who's going to open the door to me the first time I knock, and say yes, sure, I can go out on to their balcony and take a few pictures.'

'Yes, sure,' he echoed.

'Yes, sure! You better believe it!' She whirled around again, and made for the lift.

'Lady, if you're a journalist you ought to listen. The door's open.'

Listen? She always listened! And what had he said?

'Oh,' she muttered.

He waited until she had retraced her steps to his doorway. Then the narrow gaze cracked open into a slow, wide, oddly seductive smile.

And with it her eyes connected with a pair of startlingly clear grey eyes, set under heavy black brows.

Curse it, thought Claire, he was not only maddening, he was also maddeningly attractive! And boy, did he know it!

She'd chosen a risky way of setting about getting her picture, she thought uneasily—and not for the first time. Knocking on strange men's doors wasn't her style, not at all. But it was so important to her that she get this particular shot right, and after days of prowling around the bay she hadn't been able to make out any other spot where she would be able to take it from. It was a calculated risk, and not a particularly large one, but she would have felt a great deal more comfortable if a middle-aged woman, say, had opened her door.

'Coming in?'

'Well, thank you. That is, I—er...'

'I'll leave the door open,' he added, 'so you can cut and run if you feel the urge.'

Feel the urge? She felt it already! Calm down, Claire, she told herself. This is the chance you need; don't blow it now through a stupid attack of nerves.

She slid past him and into the room, awkwardly, since he showed no inclination to move and she was absolutely determined that she wouldn't brush up against that expanse of bare tanned flesh, even in the most casual of ways. Then she paused, orientating herself. A standard hotel room, plusher than many, with two double beds strewn with an assortment of male possessions. And, at the far end of the room, sliding glass doors that surely gave out on to the balcony.

'This is very kind of you,' she said nervously. 'I'll try not to keep you too long. I'll just go out on to the balcony and take my pictures, and...'

'No sweat. Take your time. Want a beer?'

'Oh. Thank you, but no, I really don't mean to...'

'Cool you down. It's a hot morning.'

Claire didn't answer him. One of the glass doors was already open; she made her way through it, and on to the balcony. This was it, she knew it straight away—exactly the view she had been looking for. With a normal lens she would be able to get almost all of the bay into a single shot; with a wide angle she could probably fit in some of the mountains beyond as well.

It was later in the day than she would have chosen—she wouldn't have knocked on doors at dawn—but the air was clear and the light perfect. This was exactly what she wanted: nothing tricksy, nothing over-dramatic, just a good, clear picture of the bay to illustrate her article. She set her camera bag down on one of the pair of slatted chairs that were the balcony's only furniture, and began to rummage for her light meter.

'Mind it straight from the can? I'm a bit short of glasses, but I can maybe track down a toothmug if you're picky.'

Of course he wouldn't leave her alone, curse him—that was too much to expect. He would hang around, wouldn't he, watching her set everything up, distracting her when she was trying to fix her focus, asking dumb questions at the wrong moment. She glanced up in sheer annoyance. But somehow the annoyance evaporated at the sight of a casually competent male, ripping the pullring off a can of lager, and handing it over with that disconcerting smile of his.

He was right, it *was* hot, and the combination of the dusty walk down from her own little guest house a hundred yards inland, and the nervous business of knocking on doors, had made her decidedly sweaty and uncomfortable.

'That's fine. Thanks a lot.'

'Shout out if you need any help.'

Wonder of wonders, he went indoors again. Claire paused for a moment to take a good slug of the beer. It was very cold; he must have a fridge in the room, she thought. Then she set down the can and got to work.

Fifteen minutes or less, and it was all finished: a dozen different shots, all taken at slightly different angles and with varying exposures, to make absolutely sure that she would have one that was right for the piece. She replaced the lens cap, set the camera back in its case, and zipped up the bag. Then she paused for a moment, and glanced again at that view. Before then she had needed to assess it professionally, for its photogenic qualities; now she could afford to admire it for itself.

And glorious it was, too: the sea, a deep azure, the pale, almost white sand of the beach, the pretty colour-washed cottages of the village, the bobbing fishing-boats in the little harbour at the other side of the bay, and the jagged peaks that acted as backdrop. No wonder this place was being developed as a tourist resort, in spite of its distance from any centres of population.

'Next year, of course, it'll all be ruined.'

He was back, right at her side. But strangely, she wasn't annoyed: it was so relaxing to be standing there gazing at the idyllic view that she couldn't have worked up any real exasperation with him if she'd tried.

'Ruined? But it couldn't be.'

He gave a low grunt, almost like a sad laugh. 'Could easily, honey. Stand at the other side of the bay, and what do you see? The same sea, the same beach, the same mountains—and this damn great hotel, dumped right in the middle of it all.'

'Well, I know it's a cheat, in a sense, that we're standing inside the hotel and don't have to look at it. But all the same——'

'All the same, there'll be another hotel next year, twice as large, over on the other side of the bay above the harbour. See the blue-washed house over there, right behind the café? It'll be on that site to the right of it, going out towards the sea. A thousand-roomer.'

'But in a year? In a year, surely——'

'Takes less time than that, these days. No planning departments in a place like this; there's only the Department of Tourism officials to bribe, and it's all fixed. The plans are drawn up already. I'll show you them, if you like.'

Claire glanced at him. 'You mean that you——'

'I didn't say I like it, honey. Just that that's how it's going to be.'

'Well, it shouldn't! And if you have anything to do with it——'

'If you're taking pretty pictures of this place, and publishing them, you're as much to blame as I am.'

He said this in a calm, decisive voice that neither accepted nor denied her criticism, merely deflected it, damn him! And he did so accurately, too. Her article wasn't designed to wreck this tranquil bay, it wasn't even particularly designed to bring more tourists out here but, simply by showing how beautiful the place was, it would almost certainly have that effect. The very people who read her words and admired her pictures would probably end up staying in his new hotel on the other side of the bay.

His hotel. He'd virtually admitted he was something to do with the planned hotel, but what? Claire stole a surreptitious glance at him. She had been too nervous earlier to glean much more than a general impression of a muscular, well-tanned male body, but now she noticed that, though the shorts he wore were tattered cut-offs, his wristwatch was a Rolex. There was something sharply decisive about the jut of his chin, in spite of the short stubble that covered it. He had an air of authority about him. From his physique he might have been a labourer; but no, not this man, staying in this hotel.

He turned his head just then, and his steely eyes connected with hers.

'Jake Eagleton,' he said, holding out the hand which didn't clasp his lager can.

Claire took it. His grip was firm and confident, his hand cool and dry.

'Claire Middleditch.'

'A photo-journalist. Should I know the name?'

'Oh, no.' Claire gave a nervous laugh. 'I'm a very new photo-journalist, I'm not famous or anything.'

'Your first assignment?'

It was her first really big assignment, and absolutely the first job for which she had ever travelled abroad, but she wasn't going to admit that to him. 'Of course not.'

'Where have your pieces been published?'

In the school newspaper, Claire thought to herself. And there had been a few pictures in small-circulation magazines, and the odd little article for the local weekly paper; but there had been nothing on the scale of this before. She had never even thought of being a full-time journalist, let alone of doing this kind of work, before she had won the *Sunday Tribune*'s competition a couple of months earlier.

'Oh, here and there,' she said as airily as she could. 'Look, thanks a million, Mr Eagleton, for the loan of your balcony. Buy the *Sunday Tribune* in six months or so, and maybe you'll recognise the picture in the colour supplement.'

'The *Sunday Tribune*? That's a pretty good paper.'

'I'll tell the editor you think so. And thanks again.'

'Not so fast,' Jake Eagleton drawled.

Claire hadn't noticed him moving, but somehow he seemed to be blocking her path to the open section of the glass door from the balcony. There was nothing threatening about his attitude, but there was something quietly decisive about it that told her he didn't intend her to leave yet.

'You haven't finished your lager,' he said.

'So I haven't.'

'Then grab a chair, and get some sun while you down it. And you can drop that frightened-rabbit look. I'm not about to leap on you.'

Frightened rabbit? What an appalling man he was! Though it was true, Claire thought; she was unnerved, and probably did come across as edgy. She wasn't the kind of girl who generally went around knocking on strangers' doors and asking to take photographs; she had always led a very sheltered life. It had taken all her courage to do it in the first place, and that had been

before she had known it would be Jake Eagleton's door
that she knocked on!

'I hadn't meant to disturb you any more,' she said
weakly.

'Lady, you disturbed me half an hour ago. I'm wide
awake now.'

'You mean you weren't? But it was half-past eleven
when I knocked!'

'And I was still getting over one hell of a night.' Jake
Eagleton grinned at her, then gazed down at the can of
lager. 'You know what they say,' he murmured. 'Never
stop drinking, and you never get a hangover.'

He drank. Claire watched him, fascinated. She didn't
approve, not at all, but there was something that caught
at her senses in the sight of his hard, muscular body,
the lazy ease with which he moved, the directness of his
gestures. One hell of a night. Where had he spent it, she
wondered, and with whom?

She wasn't used to men like him, all steel and flint
and masculine power. She wasn't used to sitting on balconies in the hot sun with dangerous strangers. The sun,
the balcony, the man and the situation: all of it radiated
excitement. She had come on this assignment in the
search of some excitement, but right now she couldn't
help thinking how very far she was from home, and from
the comforting safety of all that was familiar to her.

How far she was from Philip. She had never seen
Philip wearing as few clothes as Jake Eagleton was
wearing now. Would he look like this, she wondered
suddenly, all rippling muscles and smooth skin dusted
with dark, curling hair? If it were Philip sitting next to
her on the balcony, would she be as disturbingly aware
of his maleness as she was of Jake Eagleton right now?

That wasn't a comfortable question. She ought to go. She ought to finish her beer—she had to, for politeness' sake, now she had crashed in on his morning—and then get moving. She reached for her own can.

'You staying here for long?'

'No. No, I'm leaving in the morning.'

'Have dinner with me tonight.'

It wasn't even a suggestion, more of a cool, arrogant statement.

'I really don't think I——'

'Where are you staying?'

'In a guest house up beyond the main square.'

'Give me the address. I'll pick you up at eight.'

Claire opened her mouth to protest, but somehow the words didn't come out right. She gazed at him, somehow thinking that the sight of him would persuade her that this was totally impossible, but his cool grey gaze told her quite the opposite. This was not only possible, this was fixed.

She told him the name of the little hotel, and he nodded. 'I'll be there. And now I'd better get moving, I've work to do.'

He picked up the lager can, and gave it a shake to make sure it was empty. From the way in which he held it, Claire half thought for a moment that he would simply hurl it over the edge of the balcony, and out to the sea. But no, he stood up, still holding it, and reached for her empty can. He disappeared through the doors with the two cans. Claire got up and followed him.

'You know your way out.'

'Er, yes...'

'See you tonight.' The wide, warm, lazy smile came back to his face, and Claire found her own expression answering it.

'Yes, tonight.'

In a daze, she made her way back to the corridor, and to the lift. It wasn't until she had passed through the crowded hotel lobby and out on to the promenade, that she stopped and slapped her hand to her face and thought, what have I fixed myself up with?

A date, that was what. Practically a blind date, with a man she had barely met and knew absolutely nothing about. Claire Middleditch, she thought, what on earth do you think you are doing? What would her mother and father say? What would Philip say? She was practically engaged to Philip, and it didn't take much thought to tell her that if he ever found out that she had had dinner with another man he would be shocked.

Philip was easily shocked. As a doctor, he always behaved irreproachably, avoiding any situation which held the remotest risk of gossip or scandal, and he expected Claire to do the same. But he was hardly likely to find out, Claire reminded herself, since he was more than a thousand miles away from her. And there wasn't any reason for him to be shocked; none at all. This wouldn't really be a date, it was more in the line of a business encounter. She would only be showing her gratitude to Jake Eagleton for allowing her to use his hotel balcony— and hopefully passing a pleasant evening with him.

It wasn't the sort of thing she would have done back home, admittedly, but the whole point was that she *wasn't* back home. She was on a great adventure, the start of a new career, and it was time to do things that she wouldn't normally have done. Why not have dinner with Jake Eagleton? she asked herself, more confidently. It would be a great improvement on another lonely evening spent in her hotel room. Surely practised international photo-journalists didn't spend their evenings alone in hotel rooms? Surely they took up this kind of casual invitation without thinking twice about it?

He hadn't meant it as a romantic assignation, Claire told herself, just as a friendly gesture. He certainly wasn't a crazy rapist, she had already been into his hotel room and emerged unscathed, though she wouldn't be so rash as to go back to his room if he were to invite her there again. No, she would just spend a pleasant evening with him, enjoy a shared meal and an interesting conversation, and then say goodbye and go back without any regrets—or any guilt—to Philip and Winterton.

And, just to make absolutely sure that he didn't get the wrong impression, she would tell him about Philip, she told herself, as soon as he called for her that evening.

CHAPTER TWO

BY five to eight that evening, Claire was sitting in the little bar below her guest house, with a half-empty glass of lemonade in front of her, and a stomach that seemed to be full of fluttering butterflies.

At two minutes to eight, Jake Eagleton appeared. She saw him walk past the window, she watched him reappear, silhouetted against the evening sky, in the open doorway. She saw him make her out against the shadows of the bar, and walk over to her.

'Hi,' he said, with his easy smile. 'Want another of those?'

'It's lemonade.'

She expected a sarcastic comment, but it didn't come; he simply ordered another lemonade and a beer, and sat down opposite her.

He was fully dressed now, in pale linen trousers and a light blue shirt; casual, but smart enough for anywhere in the little village. He had shaved; there was a freshly showered look and smell about him. Clothed, he looked older than she had thought him at first: thirty at least, perhaps even in his late thirties. She could see laughter-lines drawn deep around his eyes, and a faint dark shadow below them. He wasn't on holiday here, she thought to herself. In spite of his laid-back manner and his late rising that morning, she suspected that he had really been working hard.

'Tell me about your assignment here,' he said.

'Oh, it's nothing special. Just a photo feature on the island and the resort.'

'A travel piece.'

'More or less. You know the sort of thing—somewhere exotic for your next holiday. The editor reckons this is going to be the new trendy place to go.'

'Heaven preserve it,' Jake said sardonically. 'You do this sort of thing all the time?'

'Not exactly.'

She hadn't meant to tell him about the competition, or Mrs James and her boutique, where she had worked ever since leaving school, or any of it, really. She hadn't expected him to ask. With Philip, she never talked much about her own life; it was always him, his day's work—in as far as he could tell her about it without giving away his patients' confidences—and his plans for his career. But Jake's interest wasn't as superficial as she had expected it to be; he questioned her carefully for a long time, about everything she had seen and done.

'Sounds like you've done a thorough, professional job,' he said at last. Their glasses were empty; outside, the stars were coming out in the dark expanse of sky that stretched over the bay.

'I reckon I have,' Claire agreed. 'It's the best break I'm ever likely to get, and I feel that I really wouldn't deserve to make a decent career if I hadn't put everything I had into it.'

'And that really matters to you? Building up your career?'

'Of course it does.'

He nodded his approval of her response. 'All the same,' he said, 'you were a damn fool this morning.'

'Damn fool? But I planned out exactly how to get those shots, and I had to have them——'

'And they weren't worth the risk,' Jake cut in easily.

'There wasn't any risk! It wasn't——'

'Sure there was.' His voice was quiet, but it oozed authority; it wasn't to be argued with, that tone. 'It was stupid of you, worse than stupid, to go knocking on strangers' doors. You never know what's lying in wait behind them.'

'But it was something I had to do, to get the right picture! It's not as if it was easy for me, going knocking like that. But I had to get the pictures right, and——'

'Claire,' Jake said, 'OK, you want to get away from the drudgery of that little shop, and be a professional photo-journalist. And OK, so with the rest of the assignment I can believe you did the best job anyone could do. But that isn't what it means to be professional, to go taking crazy risks like that. And it is a risk, too much of a risk, for a girl on her own to go hunting out strangers for whatever reason. A pro knows what he can't do, as well as what he can. He plans to survive safely, first of all.'

'Just because I'm a girl——'

'Just because you're a girl,' he agreed, coolly taking the wind from her sails. 'And if you were my girl, I'd have made damn sure before you set out that you knew better than to take that foolish kind of risk.'

'Well, I'm not your girl!'

'No, you're not.' He got to his feet, unhurriedly. 'I'm not dumb, I can tell you've got a guy back home. You've been shouting it out at me all along. Come on, it's getting late. Let's go get something to eat.'

Shouting it out at him? Shouting it out? What did he mean? Maybe she had meant to tell him about Philip straight away, but she certainly hadn't got around to it yet. Jake Eagleton saw a lot, she thought uneasily. He wasn't the kind of blind, insensitive man who misread every body message a woman sent out; he caught even the ones she wasn't conscious of. That was an unnerving thought.

'Where are we going?' she asked, as she stood up. 'Back to the hotel?'

'No. The food there's nothing special, standard tourist stuff. There's a place down by the harbour where I ate a couple of evenings ago that does some decent seafood. You haven't been down there, have you?'

'Not in the evenings.' She wouldn't have ventured out after dark to eat on her own; all her dinners had been taken at the guest house.

'That's what I reckoned. Let's go.'

He walked at an easy pace, not ambling, but not hurrying her along either. He didn't touch her, even to take her arm, but she was very conscious of his lean body moving parallel to hers.

Foolish risks, she thought. Maybe he was right, it *had* been a little rash of her to act as she had. But it wasn't fair to suggest that Philip was responsible, that he had somehow encouraged her to do it. That hadn't been the case at all. Philip couldn't have been more insistent in his disapproval of her assignment.

She didn't want to tell Jake Eagleton that.

It was only a short walk down to the harbour. It wasn't a busy harbour: a dozen small fishing-boats were moored in the shallow water, and there were just a couple of small restaurants, grown up to serve the tourists from the hotel presumably, interspersed with the fishermen's cottages along the front. Jake headed confidently for the further one. Claire hadn't had any impression that he was keeping to a deadline, and it was already much later than she usually ate, but he had booked, or at least made some kind of informal arrangement, she realised, because the waiter greeted them as if they were expected and showed them to one of the best tables, by the window overlooking the harbour.

'Can you face octopus?'

'Octopus?' Claire gave an involuntary shudder at the thought.

'OK, langoustines, then. And swordfish to follow? They do a good swordfish in tomato sauce.'

'Sounds good.' It sounded marvellous, after the tiny tough steaks and flaccid omelettes that the guest house had served up.

'And white wine. They bring the rest automatically.'

They did: chunks of white bread, hard-crusted and crumbly inside; a salad, big chunks of cucumber and tomato and onion in a very garlicky dressing; fizzy mineral water; slices of lemon, oozing with juice, to squeeze over the langoustines. The food was very fresh and very hot. The little restaurant was full, but its atmosphere was quiet. In a corner, a fisherman began to strum at a guitar, and sing in a low chanting voice.

Perfection, thought Claire: the food, the wine, the surroundings, the ruggedly handsome man sitting opposite her. This was the sort of magic moment she had yearned for back in Winterton, the sort of moment that she had imagined when she had been so determined to take the assignment. There hadn't been any other moments like this, admittedly—the rest of her time in the little resort had been decidedly lonely—but this one had certainly been worth waiting for.

'What do you do, Jake?'

'Do? I'm a structural engineer.'

She hadn't known what to expect, but somehow it wasn't this: it wasn't a job that she knew anything about.

Jake's face creased into his lazy smile. 'It's a stage beyond architecture,' he explained. 'My job is to assess sites, and decide what kind of buildings they can take, what foundations are needed, and that kind of thing.'

'So you're testing the site for the new hotel?'

'That's right. It's a tricky site. Part of it's granite-based—that's the hard rock of the mountains inland—with just a shallow soil covering, but there's a deeper layer of soil over the rest, and I have to test to make sure the foundations will be firm.'

'So this place can be ruined.'

'It'd be a damn sight more ruined if the hotel were built badly. Those are the places that really bug me: the holiday resorts where hotels were just jerry-built, and ten, even five years later they're simply falling apart.'

'You'd prefer them to be indestructible?'

'I'd prefer them to be well built. And well designed, too. But good design isn't just a matter of making a pretty picture: it's a matter of fitting buildings to their locations in every dimension.'

'On firm foundations.'

'Not least.' He grinned. 'It's a question of getting it right technically. Like your photos. There's not the slightest bit of use in fixing on a great view, unless you know how to take a picture competently. And there's no point choosing the best of sites for a building, unless you work out how it needs to be built.'

'That makes sense.'

'Sure it does. I'd take you to see the site if I had time, show you what I mean.'

'Not now.'

'No, it's too dark.'

They sat in silence for a moment, as Claire thought over what he had said.

'So you travel a lot?' she asked him.

'Yes, a lot.'

'You're not married?'

'Hell, no.' He gave an edgy laugh, as if the idea that he might be seemed ridiculous to him.

That laugh annoyed her. 'But haven't you ever... haven't you ever fallen in love?'

It was a silly question, she thought as soon as she had said it. He would probably think her soppy and sentimental, and it was too personal in the circumstances. But he didn't show any annoyance. He just raised his brows a fraction, and said in his lazy, level voice, 'Falling in love's a loser's game, Claire. Lust, yes. Everyone gets hit by that sometimes. But I learned early on that the ones who travel fastest are the ones who travel alone.'

'That's an awfully cold philosophy.'

'Maybe I'm a cold man.' He said this abruptly, almost offhandedly, and went on to add, 'More coffee?'

'Please.'

They sat in silence over the coffee, listening to the guitarist and the gentle hum of voices around them. Strange, thought Claire: she had thought him antagonistic, almost aggressive at the hotel that morning, but just then he didn't strike her as cold at all, but as a very warm person, and the easiest of company. They drank a third coffee too. She didn't want to move and break up the lovely evening, and it seemed that he felt the same way.

Finally the little restaurant began to empty. The guitarist and his friends departed, and the waiters began to clean up the empty tables.

'Come on,' said Jake. 'I'll walk you back to your hotel.'

He took her hand as they made their way out on to the quiet quayside. The moored boats were flooded in moonlight, the sea shone silver. As if by unspoken agreement, they made their way to the water's edge.

'A perfect place,' Claire whispered.

'Not really. There are political troubles; the whole government is riddled with corruption; the army's practically out of control, and the economy's sunk back in the nineteenth century.'

'But it looks it, tonight.'

'It looks it tonight,' he agreed.

She stared out for a moment at the harbour. Not a boat was moving, not a light flickered on the hills beyond the village. It was unnervingly quiet, even for a paradise, or a place that seemed so in the moonlight. Then she turned and looked at Jake. His eyes were fixed on the harbour too, and on his face was an odd expression, which seemed to combine the cynicism with which he had spoken a moment earlier with an almost poetical joy in the beauty of the scene.

There seemed a sweet inevitability about it when he too turned round, and met her eyes. His eyes were almost black in the darkness. They were almost on a level with hers: she was a tall girl, and he was only an inch or so taller.

He held her look for a long moment, and then he moved his face towards hers, and very softly, his lips brushed hers.

Claire felt as if she had been hypnotised by his look, his touch. The light kiss hadn't dispelled the aura of expectation that seemed to surround them: it simply intensified it. They stood there for a moment, eyes locked once more, then Jake's arms came out and surrounded her, and his mouth came down on hers again, this time with a firmness that gradually intensified until her lips parted under the pressure, and his tongue invaded her mouth.

Her response wasn't considered, it was instinctive. But there was nothing familiar about the sensations his kiss stirred in her. A ripple of pleasure seemed to snake its way down her body, from lips to chest to toes. And to the fingers that moved, as if of their own accord, to roam across the broad expanse of his back. She could feel his flesh, faintly warm beneath the soft material of his shirt; she was conscious of the faint, rhythmic thud of his heart.

Then he was releasing her, slowly and unhurriedly, his mouth and hands and arms and fingers all relaxing their grip until they stood an uncertain half-pace apart, their breathing a little ragged against the quiet of the evening.

'You don't love him, do you?'

For a moment Claire didn't understand what he was saying. 'Love who?' she echoed, confused.

'The guy back home.'

'Don't love him? What, just because I let you kiss me? You arrogant, self-satisfied, over-confident...'

'Not just because of that,' Jake said calmly. Claire saw the flicker of a half-smile in the darkness. 'Though that helped to tell me. It's the way you didn't mention him once, all through dinner. The way you dress. Even the way you go about doing the kind of things he wouldn't want you to do. All that tells me you don't love him.'

'Then it tells you wrong,' Claire said grouchily.

'Could be. I'm wrong sometimes.' He gave her his ironical smile again. And said, in a low voice, 'You going to marry him?'

'Some day.'

'And keep on flying off on your own, doing this kind of assignment?'

That was a mean question to throw at her, especially when she had been knocked off balance by his kiss. Claire's interest in photo-journalism had already caused several rows with her parents, who had pointed out to her very firmly that it wasn't a career that would fit in well with marriage and motherhood. But that was an old-fashioned attitude, she had argued: modern women *did* manage to combine career and homemaking, even if it wasn't always easy. Modern men, men of her generation, surely accepted that—even if they did grumble sometimes, as Philip had certainly done when she took this assignment!

'If I can get more assignments like this, yes.'

'What does he do?'

'He's a doctor. A general practitioner.'

'That figures. Friend of the family?'

'My father's junior partner.'

Jake nodded. He was reacting almost as if he had known this all along, Claire thought uncomfortably. He seemed to be able to read her mind with disturbing ease.

'And he's encouraging all this? Your jetting around the world?'

Claire frowned. She didn't want to discuss Philip with Jake, especially if he was going to be so aggressive, so damnably good at finding the weak points in her plans.

'He knows all about my ambitions.'

'Sounds to me like a recipe for trouble. Especially when you don't love him.'

'But I didn't say I didn't——'

'OK, drop it.' Jake turned from her, abruptly, and set off towards the road that led to the main square. Claire stood watching him for a few seconds, then she pushed her feet into action, and followed him. He was walking slowly, and in fifty yards or less she had caught up with him.

They walked on in silence for a while, then he said, quite suddenly, 'You don't truly know what you want out of life, do you, Claire?'

'I don't understand what you mean.'

'I reckon you do,' he quietly corrected her. 'OK, I know, you want it all. You want marriage and babies and the whole velvet trap; and you want a career, you want to see the world and make a name for yourself as a photo-journalist. But you're not that dumb. You surely realise you can't have them both.'

'I don't see why not.'

'Then you haven't thought it through properly.'

'I have! It's you who's not thinking, who's bringing out all the old stereotypes! You make it sound as if I've got to make a clean choice between marriage and a career. But it isn't like that for women these days. That's a really old-fashioned, male chauvinist attitude.'

'To think you can't have it all?' Jake gave a weary grin. 'That's not male chauvinism, that's experience, honey. Maybe with some jobs you can do them both. But not with yours, nor mine either.'

'That's just not so! Lots of men have jobs that mean they have to travel, and they still get married and raise families. I know what it is, Jake Eagleton. You're just plain jealous! You haven't married yourself, and it's got so you've told yourself you never could have done. And when somebody tells you you're wrong, that really bugs you, doesn't it?'

'When someone's as blind as you are, that bugs me. You know any of those guys, Claire? The guys who travel and leave their wives and kids at home? You know any happy marriages that run on those lines? Because I've seen plenty of marriages like that, I can tell you, and I could count on the fingers of my third hand the ones that are happy. And for the woman to do the travelling—hell, that'd be a thousand times worse!'

'It would be hard, I don't deny that. But whoever said that life ought to be easy? You have to work to get the things that are worth while. I reckon I could manage it, if I really worked at it.'

'Married to a doctor? A man who's tied to one spot, who works himself until he drops and then expects to come home to a hot supper and a warm bed at the end of every day? If he thinks for a moment it would work, he's an even bigger fool than you are! If you loved him like crazy, and he you, it would still be more than either of you could carry.'

'I do love him!'

'Not in the right kind of way you don't, or you wouldn't have responded to me as you did!'

'I only kissed you, for heaven's sake!'

Jake suddenly stopped still in the middle of the path, grabbing at Claire's arm and yanking her to a halt, too.

'You only kissed me?' he said, in a low, almost menacing voice. 'No, you didn't, Claire. I kissed you. And you kissed me back, and then I stopped. Now, you just think for a moment about what would have happened if I hadn't stopped. You think about what would have happened if I'd decided I wanted you in my bed tonight, and set about getting you there. If I'd kept on kissing you, and then I'd started more than kissing you, and you'd kept on enjoying it as much as you were doing back there. You think about what would have happened then, and what that would have done to your re-

lationship with your doctor back home. You think about
it.'

'How dare you suggest that? I'm not that kind of a
girl, I——'

'What kind of girl? Oh, you're not promiscuous, I
can see that. If you were, I most likely wouldn't have
stopped. But I'll tell you this, Claire, and you'd better
believe me. If I hadn't stopped, you wouldn't have been
able to stop me. And I don't mean I'd have raped you,
either. I could have had you begging me to make love
to you.'

'You rude, arrogant, egotistical——'

'You want me to prove it?'

He didn't wait for her to answer the question. The
hand that was still holding her by the arm suddenly pulled
her hard against him, and his other arm moved around
her back to pin her there. He held her like this, locked
firm in his arms, for a long, taut moment. Then his
mouth came down on hers again, this time with a force
that wasn't controlled as it had been before, but raw and
naked and shatteringly powerful.

Claire was furious! Her anger at him pulsed through
her, and she struggled convulsively against him. But even
her strongest efforts didn't seem to make any impression
on him at all. And the touch of his mouth, his hands,
the feel of his strong body pressed hard against hers,
were all making an all-too-powerful impression on her
senses. Her fury seemed to melt away in the furnace of
his sensual attack. Her body was turning into a limp,
molten mass. It seemed to reshape itself involuntarily,
fitting closely, perfectly against his.

Slowly, the powerful grip of his hands was trans-
formed into a sensuous caress. Slowly, the pressure of
his mouth eased. It wasn't attacking her now, it was se-

ducing her into responding to him. And, curse it, she couldn't help responding. When his mouth moved, and he began to trace kisses down her jawline, down her neck, in the hollow of her collarbone, she opened hers to protest, and all she could manage was a groan of sheer pleasure.

No sooner had this escaped her than he let her go, so abruptly that she had to grab on to him herself in order to avoid falling.

'Believe me now?' he asked huskily.

Oh, she believed him. The lesson had struck home, all right. But it wasn't a lesson that she wanted to learn. She loosed her grip sharply, and took a shaky step backwards.

'Don't you ever touch me again,' she whispered unsteadily.

'I shan't.'

He turned away from her as he said this. 'Come on,' he added a moment later. 'I can't leave you here.'

That was true, though they were only a few yards from the guest house. Claire took a deep breath, and started walking towards it. She didn't let herself glance at Jake as he fell in by her side.

Finally they reached the door to the bar. It was very late; the door was shut, the bar closed for the night.

'Goodnight.'

'Goodnight,' Claire grudgingly responded. He didn't move, and she added, awkwardly, 'Thanks for the supper.'

'I'll look out for the article.'

'OK.'

'Take care.'

He paused for a moment more, looking intently at her in the dim light, almost as if he was memorising her appearance. And then he was gone, vanishing into the darkness of the square.

Take care, thought Claire. Take care. It was an oddly gentle farewell, following on the disturbingly powerful scene a few moments earlier.

The door to the guest house was locked, and she fumbled in her pocket for the key. Inside, there was just one faint light glowing behind the closed bar, showing her the way up the stairs. She made her way up in the gloom, unlocked the door to her room, and groped for the light switch.

There was only a feeble bulb, cheaply shaded, to light the room, but after the darkness it seemed startlingly bright. There was her case, thrown on the bed, half packed with the things she had put in before she had gone out that evening. A damp towel, thrown over the back of a chair. And on the little bedside-table, the photographs that she carried with her everywhere: one of her mother and father, and one of Philip.

It suddenly seemed vitally important that she should look at these photographs. She picked them up, one in each hand, and stared at them in the flickering light.

He travels fastest, Jake had said, who travels alone. But that is a man's philosophy, thought Claire; the women of this world simply cannot do that.

She already had her ties. A firm and unbreakable tie to her parents, and a commitment, too, to live the kind of life that would be acceptable to them. Her marrying Philip would suit her parents perfectly. They would have her close at hand, and she them; they would gain a son-in-law they liked and admired; and they could look forward to the grandchildren that they both longed for.

Her eyes lingered longest on the photo of her parents, and then moved on to Philip's picture almost reluctantly, as if she felt awkward about facing him, even on paper, after the unnerving encounter with Jake Eagleton.

It was a good picture, one taken by a photographer on the local newspaper to illustrate a little piece about the town's new doctor. Philip was a handsome man, in a quiet, undemonstrative sort of way. With his lean face and regular features, he looked pleasant and reliable, the kind of doctor any woman—or man—would be glad to find sitting behind the desk in a consulting-room. And he was exactly that, Claire told herself. He was an admirable man in every way.

She loved him, of course she did. They had been going out together for almost two years; they had been planning on a formal engagement the following Christmas. It was true that Philip didn't stir her as Jake had, that his kisses had never had the same shattering effect on her equilibrium. But that hadn't been love, surely? Jake Eagleton didn't believe in love. It had been lust, no more. Hadn't he said so himself?

Lust or not, it had been disturbing, frightening almost in its intensity. Claire didn't like to put into words her instinctive knowledge that Jake had been telling the truth: that if he had wanted her as a mistress, she would have been hopelessly incapable of refusing him. It didn't fit with her picture of her life, of the difficult but exciting future she was trying to forge for herself.

It really would be impossible to combine marriage and travel, if she kept on coming across men like Jake Eagleton. But she had never met a man before who had had such an effect on her; so perhaps, she thought to herself, she would never meet one again. She certainly wouldn't see any more of Jake, since she was, thank goodness, leaving the resort first thing in the morning. There was only one thing for her to do. Forget him.

* * *

It was very late when Claire finally went to bed. The little room was quiet, the evening pleasantly cool, the bed not too uncomfortable, but even so she found it hard to sleep. It was easy to tell herself to forget about Jake, but somehow her mind simply wouldn't obey her.

Finally she drifted off into an exhausted sleep. She wasn't conscious of anything more until she heard the rapping of the chambermaid at the door of her room the next morning.

Wearily, Claire reached across for the wristwatch she had left on her bedside-table. She pulled it down to her, and glanced at the face.

Eight o'clock. *Eight o'clock!* But she had meant to wake at seven, to give herself plenty of time to get to the airport for the nine-thirty flight!

And she had been so obsessed with the thought of her date with Jake, she scolded herself, that she had clean forgotten to change the time of her regular morning call. She leaped out of bed, grabbed at her thin wrap, and dashed down the corridor to the little shower-room.

Half an hour later, breakfastless but fully dressed, she was clambering into a taxi and giving the driver instructions to dash to the airport as fast as possible. Hardly necessary, she thought ruefully, as she clung to her seat while he revved up alarmingly and swung round the corner to the airport road. Everyone in this place seemed to drive like a maniac, and to know no speed other than flat out.

She was confident that she wouldn't miss the plane. She would be late boarding, perhaps, but it was a little airport, with few formalities; they wouldn't bar her from the flight because of that. In less than an hour she would be on her way back home. And then it would be time to write up her notes, to develop her photos, to send in her assignment, and to plan how she might take the next steps along the path that led to her future.

What would Jake be doing? she wondered. Going over his hotel site again, perhaps, or getting ready to move on to another job in a far-flung part of the world. During her quick shower her mind had settled with irritating persistence on one of his remarks the evening before. The way she dressed, he said, had told him that she didn't love Philip. Why? How? It wasn't as if she had dressed to seduce him. The cotton frock she had worn the evening before hadn't been provocative: the material wasn't transparent, the neck was quite high, the skirt fairly long. She couldn't understand what he had meant.

Nor was she ever likely to find out now. She was leaving Jake Eagleton behind her, with everything else in this place. She was going home.

With a final squeal of brakes and screech of misused tyres, the taxi bounded to a stop outside the airport terminal building. Claire glanced at her watch. Five to nine—tight, but not impossible. She hastily shoved a pile of notes into the driver's hand, grabbed her case, her camera bag and her holdall, and ran for the check-in desk.

'Any chance of an aisle seat?' she asked the airline representative.

'So sorry, madam. There's only one flight to Paris today, and it's fully booked. Almost all the passengers have checked in already. I can offer you a seat here, at the front of the plane; or one here, near the back. That's all there is left.'

'I'll take the back,' Claire said quickly.

'That's the non-smoking area, right? Seat 31A.'

Claire collected her boarding-card, and hurriedly followed the girl's directions to the departures area. Her flight was already boarding; no time to grab a sandwich or buy a newspaper. She would have to hope the airline food wasn't too disgusting—or too insubstantial.

Through passport control, through a quick but thorough security check, and on to the tarmac, following the directions of the airport staff. The stewardess greeted her at the top of the steps to the plane, and pointed out the empty seat waiting for her. It wasn't difficult to spot it, since most of the other seats were already filled.

Claire was less than half-way down the aisle when she realised who her companion for the flight was going to be. Sitting in seat 31B, next to the empty space that awaited her, was Jake Eagleton.

CHAPTER THREE

'Hi,' Jake said. 'So we meet again, after all. Would you like the aisle seat, or the window seat?'

Claire stared at him speechlessly. Jake here! Jake next to her for the three hours of the plane journey! It was the last thing she had expected.

Her stomach did a little flip at the sight of him. He was dressed in a dark business suit now, with a grey shirt and mutely striped tie. Somehow that made him seem even more unnerving; he didn't look like a casual acquaintance she had met at a foreign resort, but like the sort of successful businessman her father sometimes invited to dinner.

He's dangerous, she thought, and I shouldn't sit next to him. Things had gone too far for comfort between them the night before, and she didn't know how to respond to him now so as to put them back on to an easy, casual basis.

'I'd recommend the aisle,' he said, prompting her. 'It's a long flight; you'll find it more convenient.'

The voice of common sense in Claire's head would have recommended the very far end of the plane. But that wasn't a possibility, since it was packed to overflowing. 'I'm booked for the window seat,' she said stiffly.

Jake opened his mouth as if to protest that she hadn't answered him, then he turned his expression into one of his familiar lazy smiles. 'Enjoy the view,' he murmured, and eased out of his own seat to let her past him.

Claire slipped into seat 31A, and stowed her camera bag and the holdall that held her personal things on the floor in front of her. She tried not to glance at Jake as he reseated himself next to her.

Perhaps he's embarrassed too, she thought. Perhaps he'll leave me alone and not talk to me any more. But she didn't really believe that he would act like a stranger, so it was no surprise when he said, 'I didn't reckon you'd be on the Paris flight, or I'd have told you that I was leaving today.'

'There is no direct flight to London.'

'That explains it. Me, I'm making for Munich.'

'Work?'

'Of course. I live in London, but I hardly ever touch base there, and this time it'll be straight on to my next assignment.'

'I see.' Claire reached for her bag. She might not have had time to buy a newspaper, but she was fairly certain that she had slipped into her hand luggage the paper-back that she had bought at the airport on the way out. She had already read all but the last chapter of it, and as the story hadn't appealed to her much she had got that far only out of sheer boredom in the evenings she had spent at the guest house. But she would start again at the beginning, she told herself, and make it occupy her for the whole three hours that it took to get to Paris. Too bad if she appeared to be rude—better that than another long conversation with Jake Eagleton.

She could sense Jake's lazy gaze fixed on her as she rummaged more and more desperately through passport, ticket, hotel and taxi receipts, make-up and the other miscellaneous contents of her bag. At last her fingers found the corner of the paperback, and she fished it out, resisting the temptation to glance at him in triumph.

'What's the book?' he asked.

She couldn't bring herself to be offensively rude to him, so she showed him the cover.

'*The Terror,*' Jake read from it. 'I read it ages ago. Wouldn't have thought it was your thing at all.'

'It isn't much.'

'I've the latest Frank Jackson, if you want to swap.'

It was a tempting offer. She liked Frank Jackson's mysteries, and she hadn't yet come across his latest, well-reviewed effort. But she didn't want to be indebted to Jake. Eagerness and reluctance fought in her, until at last she said politely, 'But you've already read this. It would leave you with nothing to read at all.'

'No sweat. I generally sleep on plane journeys.' He grinned as he said this.

'Well, if you really don't mind——'

Jake's response was to reach in his jacket pocket. Claire watched him. It was funny, she thought; she had taken him for the sort of man who lived in casual clothes and would be acutely uncomfortable when forced into a suit, but in fact he looked very good in it. It was well-fitting, and in a strange way the formal lines seemed to emphasise his quality of rugged masculinity even more forcefully than his tattered cut-offs had done.

And what did he make of her clothes? she wondered briefly. Did her beige slacks and shirt betray the fact that she didn't love Philip? Curse the man!

'Starts slowly,' he said, 'but it livens up about page fifty.'

'Thanks.'

Claire opened the book. It was that awkward dead time, when all the passengers were ready but the plane had not yet been cleared for take-off. There wasn't any real distraction to keep her from becoming absorbed in the story. Jake was certainly being careful not to provide any; he seemed to be reconciled to her wish to avoid talking to him. But just the fact of his sitting so close, the faint spicy whiff of his aftershave, the sight of his hand resting on his knee, was enough to take all her attention from Frank Jackson's carefully crafted tale.

She was determined not to let him sense that, though, so she doggedly read and reread the words on the first page until at least some of their sense sank into her brain, and turned the page over with as much nonchalance as she could muster.

Jake was chatting to a plump man in a cream suit who was sitting across the aisle, in what sounded to her to be very fluent and colloquial French. The doors of the plane banged shut, and one of the stewardesses began to make her way down the aisle, checking that all the passengers had fastened their seat-belts.

Claire watched the stewardess approach, out of the corner of her eye. She was a blonde girl, heavily made-up, and she paused to exchange a word or a joke with several of the passengers. She'll stop at Jake, Claire thought mutinously. He'll smile that lazy smile at her, and get first-class service for the rest of the flight, I bet!

Hastily she turned the page again, and buried her head still further in the book. The stewardess was almost level with them. The fat man said something that Claire couldn't translate, and Jake laughed—a deep, rich chuckle.

'Everything all right, sir?'

'Will be, when you serve me a whisky.'

'I'll try and see to that after take-off, sir. And your wife?'

Wife? Claire studiously stared at the book, and waited to see how Jake would extricate himself from that one. Easily, it proved. He simply said, 'The lady's fine,' in his casual voice, and to her relief the stewardess moved on. The address system was on now, and the pilot was beginning to welcome them on board. Ten minutes to take-off.

Those ten minutes seemed to drag forever. At last the plane began to taxi down the runway, and Claire gave up the unequal struggle with Frank Jackson's improbably wonderful hero, and stared out of the porthole instead. It was a clear day, the sun hot in a cloudless sky, so they would have a good view of the ground after they took off.

The hum of the engines turned into a roar. 'Hell,' Jake murmured in her ear, 'this bit always scares me.'

Scared him? It could hardly scare him more than it scared her, Claire thought to herself. She always felt panicky at the moment of take-off.

She didn't mean to say so, but the words came out anyway. 'It scares me, too.'

Nor did she stop him when he reached for her hand. In spite of what he had said about being frightened, his grip was as firm and cool as she remembered it. She clung on shamelessly as the plane speeded up, and the roar became a searing howl. The odds of anything going wrong always are minute, she told herself; but all the same, she knew she wouldn't be able to relax until the plane was safely cruising and the risks became even more minuscule.

It was nice, more than nice, to have Jake to cling on to. His clear grey gaze seemed to absorb all her fear and neutralise it. His touch was comforting. He had unnerved her so the evening before, but now his presence seemed genuinely reassuring.

The plane lifted off, they rose rapidly into the air, and Claire, uneasily conscious that she wasn't acting at all as she had intended, slipped her hand out of Jake's and turned back to the window.

'Watch it while you can,' Jake said from her other side. 'We'll be out over the sea in a minute.'

He was right. Already they were over the village where they had both stayed. There was the white sand, the little jumble of cottages, the row of fishing-boats, the ugly great mass of the big hotel. Then a moment later there was nothing to be seen but a flat expanse of water.

She couldn't keep on gazing at that nothingness, not even to protect herself from Jake. She turned over the book, which she had left spreadeagled on her knees, and tried to resume her reading.

Three hours, she thought. Three hours of him. But that's all, Claire; then he'll say goodbye at Charles de Gaulle Airport, and you won't ever see him again. You're going back to Winterton and Philip.

It felt like much too long—and, at the same time, not nearly long enough.

'Want a drink?' Jake asked. 'Lemonade? Scotch? Shouldn't drink on planes, I know, but I always end up doing it anyway.'

'No, thanks,' Claire said shortly.

Jake didn't comment, simply reached for the stewardess call button. It was hardly necessary, for as soon as the 'fasten seat-belts' sign had gone out the blonde stewardess had begun to make her way back towards him.

He ordered a Scotch for himself and a martini for the fat man. And Claire, feeling edgy and awkward, said

'Excuse me,' grabbed her bag, and stood up to go to the lavatory.

There were only a dozen rows of seats to negotiate, but it felt like a long way. Underneath you really are unnerved, Claire, she told herself. You didn't expect to see him again, and it threw you off balance. That dark man in the seat at the back isn't staring at you, it's just your embarrassment that makes you think he is.

All the same, she was relieved to find that there was no queue at the back of the plane, and that she could lock herself in the little cubicle straight away. She lingered there for as long as she dared, tidying up the lipstick and eyeshadow that she had slapped on in two minutes flat that morning, and then rubbing half of it off again so that Jake wouldn't notice it and think she was dolling herself up for his benefit. She unfastened the tie round her ponytail too, and combed her hair through before fastening it back again.

You'll do, Claire Middleditch, she thought, as she checked herself in the mirror. Even in this horrid artificial light you pass muster. Pleasant and ordinary. Like Philip. There's nothing to make anyone give you a second glance; and that's how you like it to be, isn't it? She flipped the fastening shut on her bag, slung it over her shoulder, and folded back the door to the cubicle.

Strange—the dark man turned round and looked at her again as she emerged. Not flirtatiously, not appraisingly; almost edgily. Rubbish, she thought; you're projecting your own nervousness on to him. Go and sit down again, and stop making a fool of yourself.

The blonde stewardess was leaning over Jake when Claire reached him, serving his whisky with many smiles and giggles and flirtatious glances. Claire tried to suppress the annoyance that rose in her at this display of feminine susceptibility. She smiled sweetly when the stewardess looked up at her, and waited patiently until Jake was served. Finally the stewardess began to wiggle her way back to the front of the plane, and Claire slipped into her window seat.

'Lousy job, being a stewardess,' Jake said, as she settled down again. 'Glorified waitress really, with particularly unsocial hours.'

'There's a little more to it than that,' said Claire, who felt, in a confused way, that she ought to come to the stewardess's defence to prove that she wasn't remotely jealous of her. 'It's a big responsibility, looking after people in a plane. Maybe it is rather routine most of the time, but if anything ever does go wrong, it's the stewardesses who get to——'

Her sentence was cut short, because Jake's hand suddenly descended on to her leg, and squeezed it hard, just above the knee. She jumped, and swung her head round to stare at him. But he wasn't looking at her, he was looking at the stewardess, who was right at the front of the plane now, next to the service area, talking to a scruffy man in jeans and a leather jacket.

'Do you mind?' Claire exclaimed.

Jake paid no attention. 'Stay here,' he said shortly. 'Don't move.' He swung out of his seat, and headed off towards the front of the plane.

Don't move? Where on earth did he imagine she was going to go? Claire thought irritably. He wasn't her man, not in any sense. Maybe it didn't exactly thrill her to see him falling over a sexy blonde stewardess, but she would hardly follow him down the aisle and haul him back to sit next to her!

If she'd had any sense, she would have picked up her book again and ignored him completely. That would have served him right, cut his arrogance down to size! But she couldn't bring herself to do that, so she watched him as he strode down the aisle, until it was blocked by another man, who stepped out in front of him when he was four or five rows from the front of the plane.

Jake didn't squeeze past the man; he stopped. He and the other man seemed to be talking. Then Jake turned round again, and headed back towards Claire.

There was an odd expression on his face. Not annoyance, exactly, or resignation, more a sort of set expression, as if he was straining every muscle to keep his look impassive. Claire couldn't understand it. What could the other man have said? What on earth was Jake up to?

There had to be simple explanation, she told herself. It was a silly and trivial incident, hardly even an incident at all. But there was something about the hard set to Jake's jaw, the tightness around his mouth, that made a chilly sensation seep through her.

'Is something wrong?' she asked, as he reseated himself.

Jake turned to look at her, and as soon as she met his eyes she knew that her gut feeling had been right. There *was* something wrong, something badly wrong.

'Keep calm,' he said in a very low voice. 'Whatever happens, you're not to leave your seat. Don't shout, don't look round. Keep your head down and do nothing, then you'll be all right.'

'All right?' Claire's voice rose automatically, but she caught the tiny gesture from Jake that ordered her to lower it, and she went on in a quieter voice, almost a stage whisper, 'What is it? Is there a problem with the plane?'

'Kind of. Nothing to panic about.'

'What kind of problem? Has an engine failed, or——'

Her voice was drowned then by the sound of the address system. There was a crackle or two, and then the pilot's voice, saying, 'Hello again, ladies and gentlemen. I'm afraid we're just entering a patch of turbulence. It may cause us a problem or two, nothing serious, but as a precaution I'm asking you to refasten your seat-belts. If anyone is not seated at the moment, would they please return immediately to their seat.'

There wasn't anyone standing except for the man who had blocked Jake's path, and he was now leaning against the bulkhead surveying the other passengers, with one hand in his pocket and the other arm loose at his side. He made no visible effort to obey the pilot's order. As Claire watched he directed his gaze right down the aisle, and Claire automatically swung her head, to see what he was looking at.

Jake's hand, connecting hard with her thigh again, brought her head back round, but not before she had glimpsed the back of the plane. Another man was standing there, at the entrance to the lavatories. It was the dark man who had unnerved her earlier with his stare.

Something was happening. Something very peculiar. The two men were there, standing up, almost as if they had stationed themselves at either end of the passenger compartment; but there was no sign at all of any of the cabin staff.

A word began to snake its way up to the surface of her mind. The word was 'hijack'. And the little chill that had trickled through her earlier turned into an icy hand that grabbed hard at her heart, and squeezed it.

'Claire,' Jake was saying in a low, firm voice. 'Claire.'

With an effort, she brought her eyes up to meet his.

'Listen to me. This is important, very important. There's nothing to be frightened of. It's a nuisance, it'll hold us up, but the chances of being hurt are tiny. We'll be fine as long as we keep our heads. But you must keep calm and do as I say. Don't look round again. However much you want to, whatever happens, don't look round again. Look at me, or read your book if you can manage to. Don't look at anyone else. Don't say anything to anyone else unless they talk to you.'

Somehow, Jake seemed to be holding her hand. Claire couldn't recall his taking hold of it, but it was a little comfort, a small good thing to set against the terror that was grabbing at her. She squeezed it tightly, almost as if she was assuring herself that he was real and solid, and managed a tiny nod.

'Good girl. We'll come through this fine. Trust me. You OK now?'

Claire nodded again.

'Now, this is important, too. If one of them talks to you, you've got to try to be polite and friendly. Act like they're on your side. Tell yourself that. They're not crazy, they're doing this for a reason. You don't have to share that reason. You don't even have to think about it. But you've got to tell yourself these guys want you safe, they want us all safe. If we get hurt, they've got problems, big problems. If we die, they die. They don't want that. They want you safe and well. Understand?'

Claire opened her mouth. Her voice came out in a tiny, unsteady croak, but it did come. 'I think so.'

'OK, that's good. I'll keep telling you, you keep on believing it. Now, if they talk to you, don't you lie to them. You don't have to agree with them, they don't expect that. But you've got to make them like you. You've got to make them like you so much that they don't want to hurt you whatever happens. You've got to tell yourself that they've got mothers and girlfriends back home, that they're regular guys like anyone else. OK?'

'OK,' Claire croaked.

'Now, do you want me to keep talking, or are you going to read your book?'

What a choice, Claire thought. What a choice! But Jake was right, she knew. The very worst thing would be for her to keep thinking about it. She couldn't afford to do that, at least until the initial surge of terror had died down. She had to keep her mind away from it and try to keep calm, as he had said.

'Keep talking. Please.'

'OK. Let me think.'

His voice caught for a moment, and the thought flashed through Claire's brain that he was stretching his own self-control to the very limits. He had seen something when he walked up the aisle, something terrifying; but somehow he had found the strength to walk back steadily, and to calm her down.

And he had enough command of himself now to go on, and say, in a voice that had none of his usual lazy ease, but that seemed level and controlled all the same, 'Let me tell you about when I was a kid. I come from the north, from a little village near Newcastle. You ever been to Newcastle? You should go there some time. It's a great city. And where I was born, this place called Whitburn, it's right on the coast, and...'

He talked on and on. All around them, things seemed quite normal. If anyone else had noticed what was going on, they were evidently managing to cope with the situation just as calmly as Jake had done.

Half a dozen rows in front of them, a man began to get up from his seat. Claire saw him bend down again, as if his wife by the window was reminding him that the 'fasten seat-belts' sign was still lit; then straighten, as if he'd insisted that he had to do something. He waved towards the man standing by the bulkhead, as if to say that if that man could ignore the pilot's ruling, so could he.

Jake's steady voice trailed to a halt, and Claire knew that he was watching too.

'Keep calm,' he whispered again to her. 'Don't react, whatever happens.'

The man was making his way down the aisle towards the front of the plane. The man at the bulkhead slowly moved forwards, and brought an arm out to intercept him.

There was a sudden shrill scream.

'Oh!' a woman shrieked. 'He's got a gun!'

A moment's total silence descended on the cabin; and then there was pandemonium, with women and children screaming, men shifting in their seats, the terrorist stalking down the aisle, brandishing a gun clearly now, in the hand that had been hidden in his pocket earlier.

'Get back!' he yelled. 'Sit down!'

The man who had stood up was already retreating, his footsteps shaky, his face ashen. Claire turned round, and saw that at the back of the plane the dark man had also drawn a gun, looking as if he was ready to fire it at any moment.

The terrorist at the front half turned, and shouted something in the direction of the cockpit. Claire couldn't hear the words, they were drowned by the noise in the cabin. There was a particular commotion in the row in front of her, where a woman seemed to have fainted. Somewhere a baby was howling; a woman was shrieking hysterically.

Suddenly there was the crackle of the intercom, and the slightly shaky tones of the pilot's voice.

'Ladies and gentlemen. Please keep calm, and *please* do not move from your seats. I repeat, do not move from your seats.'

A stewardess—not the blonde Claire had noticed earlier—emerged from the cockpit, and began to make her way down the aisle towards the screaming woman. Her hair had tumbled loose under her jaunty cap, Claire noticed, and there was a dark smudge on her cheek. She bent over the woman, trying to reassure her.

Claire held tight on to Jake's hand, and she felt a warm returning pressure from him.

'Ladies and gentlemen,' the intercom crackled again. 'This is your pilot speaking still. As you may have realised, this plane has been taken over by members of a nationalist liberation movement. There's no cause for panic. I repeat, there is no cause for panic. Please stay in your seats, and try to keep calm. Do not approach the terrorists. I repeat, do not approach the terrorists.' There was a short, sudden silence, as if the pilot had been cut off from the microphone, and then the same voice resumed. 'Correction. Do not approach the freedom fighters.'

In spite of herself, Claire couldn't help laughing. In the middle of this crisis, all the terrorists could think about was being called by a different name! She turned to look at Jake, and saw a smile on his face, too. Several people around them were also laughing, as if the involuntary joke had cracked some of the tension.

Jake leaned over to her, so that he could speak quietly above the hubbub.

'I'm pretty sure it's the FLNG.'

'The *who*?'

'The extreme Marxist group. The government tried to suppress them last year, and they went underground. You didn't research the politics during your trip?'

'No. No, I've never written about politics at all.'

'They're pretty standard revolutionaries. Haven't had much coverage in the Western media. I'd guess they want publicity mainly; maybe to bargain some of their colleagues out of gaol.'

'I see.'

'Could be worse. They're a professional outfit. It's the stray crazies who get past the security checks that cause the real hijack trouble. They make all sorts of weird demands. These guys are different. They know what they want, they know how to set about getting it.'

'Thanks a lot,' Claire whispered back with heavy irony.

'You'd better believe it, honey. Could be a thousand times worse. There's every chance we'll get off with a detour and a delay and a couple of days of misery.'

'For heaven's sake!' Claire whispered back, with some annoyance. 'It's a hijack! Don't you remember that terrible business at Entebbe, and——'

'Claire, have you got any idea how many hijackings there are each year?'

Claire frowned. 'One or two, I guess. And I can't see that we rate as lucky because we got on the flight that ——'

'In a good year, there are twenty. In bad years there were seventy or more, before they tightened up the security regulations.'

'Seventy?'

'Loads of them don't even make the headlines. The hijackers give up quietly, or they make reasonable demands and the authorities give in to them. OK?'

'Heavens, if I'd known there were that many, wild horses would never have dragged me on a plane!'

'It's still much safer than crossing a busy road. OK, you can't call us lucky, it's a lousy thing to have happened. But even now, the odds are heavily in favour of our getting out again in one piece.'

'You seem to know a lot about it.'

'I used to know a couple of stewardesses. They have hijack training, and I got interested in what they told me, so I read a book or two. The books and the instructors all say the same. Keep calm, make friends with the terrorists—sorry, the freedom fighters—and you survive it OK. I know. So trust me, right?'

'I do,' Claire whispered. It was true, she did. Maybe Jake was a virtual stranger, a man she had met for the first time the day before and had never expected to see again, but all the same she did trust him. His judgement was sharp, she had been given plenty of evidence of that the night before. He hadn't taken advantage of her susceptibility to him, even though he had made it abundantly clear that he could have done. And now, when she found herself in a situation she had never, ever dreamed of facing, it was an immense relief to be bolstered by his calm conviction. A little piece of her mind thought that he was understating the danger to try to calm her, but better that by far than the panic that many people in the plane were showing.

Already, though, the panic seemed to be abating. The woman's screams had subsided to a choking sob; the baby had stopped howling. There was a steady buzz of whispered conversations all through the cabin, and a strong feeling of tension in the air, but nobody was reacting wildly. A dangerous moment had passed, and without any disaster.

The address system came on again, and the pilot's voice, already reassuringly familiar, echoed through the cabin.

'Thank you, ladies and gentlemen. I hear you're doing fine back there. Now, just try to keep calm, and we'll all be all right. I can tell you now that our hijackers have asked me to arrange a landing in Algeria, and I've already contacted the authorities in Algiers to request permission for a put-down. I'll let you know as soon as I have some definite news. Now I'm going to hand over to one of the freedom fighters, who wants to say a few words to you.'

'This'll be the political speech,' Jake whispered.

'Do I have to listen?'

'Why, would you rather read your book?'

Claire grinned at him. In spite of the horrific situation, an odd air of normality was coming back to them. I'm not going to die yet, she thought to herself. Jake's right; we're going to be OK.

CHAPTER FOUR

IN fact Claire couldn't have understood the hijacker's speech if she had wanted to, because it was in an unfamiliar foreign language. She concentrated on the first few phrases, then shut off her mind, and let the steady drone pass over her head. Occasionally she glanced at Jake. His hand was still loosely clasping hers, and she didn't want to pull hers free, even to take hold of her book. Once he caught her glance, and turned to meet it and give her a conspiratorial little smile. We're in this together, she thought. It was a comforting thought.

Her mind drifted, unintentionally, to the subject of her stomach. She felt terribly hungry. It was hours, surely, since she had had breakfast. No, she hadn't had breakfast at all, had she? In the rush that morning it had been a choice between breakfast and a shower, and knowing from experience that the guest-house breakfasts were none too wonderful, she had opted for a shower.

She couldn't help wondering when she would next enjoy either a hot breakfast or a shower. Even a cup of coffee would have been bliss right then. She glanced at Jake's plastic glass of whisky. It was still half-full; he hadn't drunk any of it since he had first realised what was happening. She didn't want any of it herself.

Would the stewardesses serve a meal? she wondered. And when? Obviously they wouldn't do anything while the terrorist was talking over the intercom. Though few people on the plane could have understood him, everyone was keeping a respectful silence, apart from the occasional grizzle from a child.

In the row in front, the man had succeeded in reviving his wife, and he was leaning over her seat, half supporting her as she groaned gently.

Finally the terrorist's voice stopped. There was a bare five seconds' pause, and it started again. It took Claire a moment to realise that this time he was speaking in English. She strained to listen, though she found this difficult because of the thick, unfamiliar accent. There was a lot of jargon about heroic revolutionaries and the class struggle, the triumph of the oppressed and so on. It was almost as boring as it had been when she couldn't understand it.

She laid her head back against the headrest. She could just see the face of the scruffy hijacker standing against the bulkhead. He looked harassed and worried. There was him, and the dark man at the back—and how many others? she wondered. The man who was addressing them. And there would surely be at least one other man in the cockpit, keeping guard over the pilot and the rest of his crew.

The English harangue ended. Another moment's blessed silence. But, before Claire could say anything to Jake, another voice started up, speaking in French this time So there are two men in the cockpit at least, Claire thought to herself. Jake was right, when he said he reckoned this was a professional job. These men must have planned it meticulously.

When the French version ended she waited for a moment, just to make sure yet another harangue would not follow, then turned to Jake and said, 'I didn't follow it all. Are they the FN whatever?'

'FLNG. Yes, they are, or at least, an extremist group attached to the FLNG.'

'And what do they want? I didn't hear them say.'

'They didn't say. That's a standard tactic. They'll be cautious about spelling out their demands at first, because they don't want to panic us. And most of all they mustn't panic the pilot, because that would endanger all of us. My guess is that they won't say until we land in Algiers—if we get permission to.'

'Will we?'

'It's hard to say. Algiers is a popular destination for hijackers.' Jake gave a taut, edgy smile. 'Another proof that this crew have done their homework. But it's usual for the authorities to try to divert the hijackers from their chosen destination. Chances are they've tried to fix things so that some of their colleagues will get on board at Algiers. It's none too easy to smuggle arms and ammunition on to a plane these days; most hijackers rely upon getting reinforcements later. And the authorities will want to prevent that, so they would probably favour a landing almost anywhere else.'

'Maybe the hijackers know that. Maybe they're bluffing, asking to go to Algiers so really they'll be diverted to—oh, I don't know, Rome or somewhere.'

'It's possible. We'll find out in time.'

'I suppose so,' Claire agreed. She thought for a moment, then said, 'So what will happen now, do you think?'

'Wish I knew. There's a pattern of sorts to these things, but every one's a little different. The FLNG have never hijacked a plane before, as far as I know, so it's pretty much an open question. They'll maybe check our passports.'

'Check our passports? What for?'

'You can guess,' Jake said grimly. 'You've an English passport?'

'Oh, yes. My family are absolutely English, through and through.'

'Mine, too. That's OK. I don't think the English are too unpopular with this lot. It's the Americans and the Israelis who always start to sweat in these situations.'

'Why? The FL what's-it isn't against Israel, is it?'

'Not directly. But most terrorist groups are funded by the Arabs in one way or another, so if there are any Israelis on board they could find themselves used as scapegoats. You've not been to Israel? Or to anywhere else where there's trouble?'

'Not at all.' Claire forced out a shaky smile. 'A holiday on the Costa Brava was about my limit before this trip.'

'That's good. Then there are no stamps in your passport to draw their attention, and there's nothing for you to worry about.'

'Thanks very much.'

Jake must have caught an overtone in Claire's words, because he threw her a curious glance, and said, 'What's up, then? What's bugging you?'

'Bugging me?' Claire almost laughed. 'We've a hijack on our hands, and you ask what's bugging me?'

'Sure I ask,' Jake retorted. 'We're going to be here for hours, days most likely, and you've got to stay calm and keep your head all through. If something's bugging you right now, something particular, you tell me right now. Then maybe I can do something about it. That would help both of us. Hell, I don't want you itchy; I've got to sit next to you for heaven knows how long.'

'True.' Claire hesitated. 'You'll think this really stupid.'

'Nothing's stupid at a time like this. If it worries you, you tell me about it.'

'Well—to tell you the truth, I'm hungry.'

'Hungry?' In spite of his earlier words, Jake gave a loud snort of laughter.

'It's not funny!'

'I'm sorry. I know it's not. In fact, it's pretty serious. What did you eat for breakfast?'

'Nothing,' Claire confessed.

'Nothing at all? Not even a cup of coffee?'

'Well, I *was* late last night, and I forgot to change my morning call, so when I did wake up I was in a tearing hurry, and——'

'And you all but missed the plane,' Jake finished for her. 'So let's get this straight. You haven't eaten at all since we had supper last night?'

'Not a thing.'

'Do you carry food in that holdall of yours? Biscuits? An orange or two?'

'No, nothing at all. I'm not a nibbler, I need to watch my weight, and...'

'Honey,' Jake said cheerfully, 'the next few days'll slim you down a treat. Well, I can't help you myself. I don't go for chocolate and all that. Haven't so much as a stick of chewing gum on me. This needs some thought.'

'I don't suppose the stewardess would——'

'Not yet,' Jake said confidently. 'Not till after we land, most likely. The terrorists won't take the usual food routine, the trolley in the aisle and all that. It's too dangerous from their point of view. She'd bring you a snack maybe if you were fainting from hunger, but you'll not get a meal out of her yet. Let me just ask around.'

'I could wait a while. I'm not really desperate yet. Perhaps in an hour or two...'

'Better try now,' Jake said. 'Most people haven't thought it out yet, they haven't faced up to how hungry they'll be at this time tomorrow. We're more likely to get something out of someone now.'

He turned to the fat Frenchman on the other side of the aisle, and began talking to him in the fast, fluent French he had used earlier. The Frenchman responded with a torrent of language and quite a few hand gestures so dramatic that Claire feared they would attract the hijackers' attention. Jake spoke some more, his voice low, almost caressing. And wonder of wonders, the Frenchman bent down and began to rummage in the carrier bag at his feet.

A minute later he emerged with a green apple in his hand. He reached over the aisle, with a gallant smile, and handed it to her.

'Er—*merci, monsieur.*'

'*Enchanté, mademoiselle.*'

Claire looked at the apple in her hand. Jake is right, she thought. By this time tomorrow we'll maybe all be ravenous. It hardly seemed fair to accept the Frenchman's apple at all, but Jake whispered, 'Eat it. Now,' and she hastily took a bite out of it.

It tasted delicious. How odd, Claire thought. We're all in a terrible predicament, and here I sit, somewhere over the sea, munching away at a stranger's apple. But what else could I do? Screaming and howling would solve nothing; it would be stupid to try any heroics in mid-air; so, as Jake says, the thing is to keep calm and concentrate on sitting it out.

'How long will it all take, do you think?'

'Hard to say. Anything from a few hours to a few days. Or even longer, if we're really out of luck. But I'll promise you this; you won't die from starvation.'

'Thank you, sir,' Claire said demurely. 'That's very thoughtful of you to tell me.'

'My pleasure,' he responded. 'In any case, we'll land, maybe at Algiers, maybe somewhere else, in the next two or three hours. The plane won't carry fuel for a flight longer than that.'

'I see.'

As if the pilot had heard Jake too, the intercom came on once more.

'I've some news for you now, ladies and gentlemen. We've been refused permission to land at Algiers, but I've put our predicament to International Air Traffic Control, and we've been cleared for a route to Tunis. It's almost ten-thirty now, and it will take us just over two hours to reach Tunis. But you'll need to put your watches back one hour, so we'll be reckoning on landing at around eleven-thirty local time.'

Almost ten-thirty? It seemed to Claire as if hours had passed already, and in fact it was barely an hour and a half since she had dashed into the airport. If it's felt like so long already, she thought, how long will it seem if the hijack drags on for two or three days, or even longer?

All the same, there was something reassuring about the normality of time zones and adjusting one's watch; and it was reassuring in a way, too, when Jake said calmly, 'Hijacked planes always get priority from air traffic control. So we can reckon to land on time; there'll be no queueing for a runway.'

'That's nice.'

'It helps a little,' he agreed.

They fell silent for a while. 'Might as well read,' Jake said. 'We've a long wait ahead of us.'

'What about you?'

He gave her a lazy smile, as if to acknowledge the change in her attitude from when they had first embarked. 'I'll get by.'

Claire picked up her book. Frank Jackson's thrilling tale seemed strangely mundane in comparison with the events that were taking place all around her. But it's peculiar, she thought, his wonderful hero never seems to have time hanging heavy on his hands—he never even pauses in his frantic action, let alone picks up a book!

Next to her, she saw Jake lean forward and pluck a pile of papers from the pocket fixed to the seat in front. He leafed his way through them—the usual safety instructions, a freebie magazine—and a moment later he nudged her, and said, 'Better take a good look at this.'

Claire looked. She had never paid much attention to the standard safety drill with life-jackets and oxygen masks, but Jake was right, she realised, it was important to them now.

Jake was drawing her attention to the diagram of the plane. 'The emergency exists are half-way down,' he said in a low voice. 'Here, and here. Look up—not too obviously. You see them? See the release handle? Go for one of those exits if it comes to a getaway. But not until I tell you, or you could get shot by mistake. And if the guy at the back moves away, there's another exit behind us. Don't look round, just check it on the plan. OK?'

'OK,' Claire agreed.

'If the military do storm the plane, don't try to run. Just get down, right down. Before we land, I want you to push your bag right under the seat in front, so there's room for you on the floor. OK?'

'OK.'

'Your shoes got stiletto heels?'

'Of course not!' Claire retorted. Then she hesitated, and added, 'Why?'

'To smash the glass in the porthole if they use gas. Not that it's likely, I don't think. Don't worry, I'll find something else.'

'All right.'

'OK, you can read again now.'

Claire did pick up the book again, but she still couldn't concentrate on the story. Everything was so disconcerting: Jake's reassuring presence, his far from reassuring instructions, the knowledge that the dark terrorist was standing just yards away from them with a gun in his hand, even the strange air of normality that the people around them had resumed. Quite a lot of them were reading now, others talking, in low, apparently calm voices.

She turned over the pages, not so much to dupe Jake, as to try to reassure him that she was coping reasonably with it all. She sensed that he was worried about her, and it pleased her.

Time passed. Near the front of the cabin a new man appeared, holding a gun and a knife. He began to make his way down the cabin, stopping next to each row of seats and checking passports. He moved slowly, so it would be some time before he reached the two of them. Claire returned to her story.

She was shaken from it again by a commotion behind her. Scuffling noises, crashes and bangs, some yells. In spite of all Jake's drilling, she couldn't help twisting round to try to see what was happening. As she did so, she felt Jake's strong arm come round her, not preventing her, just settling round her in a protective gesture.

She couldn't see much. There was a wild, almost panicky expression on the face of the dark hijacker. He was standing very still. From the front of the plane, his two companions were shouting at him. All around him, the other people were ominously silent.

'What happened?' Claire whispered to Jake. Somehow she felt confident that however little she had seen herself, he would know the answer, and be able to tell her.

He shifted a little, peering round the side of his seat and down the aisle. Then he looked back at her.

'Some damn fool had a go,' he said. 'Threw himself at the hijacker. Stupid thing to do. He could easily have scared him into firing, you can see how on edge he is. And when you get bullets whizzing round in a plane, you've got big trouble.'

'So what happened?'

'The hijacker knocked him out, from the look of it. He's lying out cold in the aisle.'

'Heavens,' Claire whispered.

The tall hijacker was coming down the aisle now, his gun cocked, his posture alert. He passed them, and knelt down beside the prone man.

'It's OK,' Jake whispered. 'He'll live.'

Claire didn't know how he could know, or even if he was telling the truth, but it was what she wanted to hear. She had somehow coped with it all so far, but she couldn't help feeling that the thought of a corpse stretched out in the aisle just behind her would be more than she could possibly bear. She turned back again, and sank into her seat, suddenly exhausted.

'It's all right,' Jake said gently. He took her hand again. 'We're still in one piece. One more bad moment behind us, that's all.'

And how many more to come? Claire couldn't help wondering.

At least there were no more incidents before they landed. The hijacker who was checking passports came to them, and trained his gun on them while he waited for them to show him their papers. Claire had never seen a gun before at close quarters. It looked smaller than she had imagined, almost like a toy gun. It wasn't the gun that was the greatest surprise to her, though, but the sweat on the hijacker's face.

He's terrified, she thought to herself. Scared stiff, much more frightened than I am. It was an oddly comforting realisation. It made the man seem human to her, in spite of his knife and gun. She remembered Jake's instructions to act pleasantly, and though she couldn't bring herself to smile when she handed over her passport, she did at least manage to do it politely.

As did Jake. There will be no wild heroics from him, Claire thought. She was glad to be confident of that. It took courage of a sort to hurl yourself at a gunman, she could see, but there was more to be said, in her opinion, for the kind of practical sense that had had Jake checking the emergency exits long before they had even landed.

At last came the announcement from the pilot that they were beginning their descent to Tunis. There was no need to refasten their seat-belts, hardly anybody had unfastened them or moved at all since the drama began.

'I'm hopeless on geography,' Claire whispered to Jake. 'Where exactly is Tunis?'

He flashed her his lazy grin—almost back to normal, by now. 'Capital of Tunisia, honey. Which is a small country in North Africa, sandwiched between Algeria and Libya. You know the bit where the African coast nicks upwards, almost like a dog's ear?'

'I think so.'

'That's where we're going. The tip of the ear, pretty much.'

'So it's near the coast?'

'All the towns in North Africa are on the coast. There's nothing but desert inland.'

'I see.' A pause. 'You seem to know everything.'

'You complaining?' he teased.

'Oh, no. Not at all.'

'I guess I've been around a fair bit.'

'You've been to Tunis before?'

'Yes.'

'Will it be hot?'

'Very. Even in the plane. Hot and stifling, and if we do get any food it'll be terrible. The whole joint will start to stink, and the passengers will start to get sick, and in a day or less the Black Hole of Calcutta would seem like a paradise compared to the inside of this plane. That what you wanted to know?'

'That's about what I figured out for myself.'

'Yeah.' Jake grinned again. 'You wanted excitement, honey, and you sure got it.'

You call this excitement? Claire thought. Sitting reading a novel in an aeroplane, waiting for something terrible to happen! The prospect of days of increasingly disgusting discomfort! Somehow, it wasn't what she had expected wild adventure to be like. Somehow she had never thought that when she got to see Africa—Africa!— she would be stuck inside an aeroplane, with only the flimsiest of chances of getting out of it in one piece. If this is the great, wide, exciting world, she thought, there's a lot to be said for getting bored stiff back in Winterton.

'Jake,' she whispered.

'Yeah?'

'I'm glad you're here.'

He glanced at her. 'You just keep on doing what I say. OK?'

'OK.'

He could have said he was glad she was there too, Claire thought irritably. She glanced at him again. He had turned away from her, and was reading a long article about the Bahamas in the freebie magazine. She could only see his profile: the firm jut of his chin, a lock of dark hair that fell forward, breaking the straight, solid line of his nose and forehead.

But he's not glad, Claire thought suddenly. How could he be? I'm glad he's here, because he's protecting me— as far as anyone can. He's telling me what to do, he's keeping me calm, he's finding me apples and making sure I know how to escape from the plane. But what am I doing for him? I'm a big, clumsy girl with a boyfriend back home, and I'm leaning on him shamelessly. And he's the kind of man who likes to travel fast and travel alone, isn't he? He probably wishes with all his heart that I hadn't got on this plane, or at the very least that I'd picked a seat at the far end of it.

It was a sobering thought—that for all the charm and courtesy he had mustered Jake Eagleton probably wished her a million miles away. So rather than talk to him again she turned to the porthole, and peered out to see if she could glimpse the coast of Africa.

Slowly, a faint and fuzzy line broke the dull continuity of the sea below them. Slowly, a coastline took shape; slowly, a town materialised; slowly, as the plane descended, Claire made out whitewashed houses, streets and cars, palm trees, and the flat-roofed buildings, wide runways and emphatic painted markings of an airport.

As they came still lower, she made out more. There were little knots of the drably painted open-backed trucks that, just about anywhere in the world, advertised the presence of troops. There were white-painted ambulances. There were flashing lights and the whole paraphernalia of an airport, not open for normal business, but on full alert for an emergency.

That's us, Claire thought. We're the emergency. The sight of those troop carriers and ambulances seemed to bring home to her, as not even the hijacker's gun had done, the extent of the danger that faced them all.

'There much to see?' Jake's voice said, from somewhere near the back of her neck.

'Sorry.' She pulled back, so that he could glimpse at least something through the porthole. 'Nothing special. Ambulances and the army. What you'd expect, I suppose.'

The fake nonchalance in her voice clearly didn't fool him.

'You get scared on landings?'

'I guess this time I am.'

'You can cling if you want to.'

She opened her mouth to say 'no', but the word didn't come out as she intended it.

'Thanks.'

He didn't wait for her to act on that; he reached over, and drew her round to face him. Claire buried her face in the dark stuff of his suit lapel. It was cool and slightly prickly. She could smell his aftershave, familiar now; she could feel his arms wrapping round her, cocooning her in at least a semblance of security. Her arms wrapped round him, too. He may not be my man for good, Claire thought, but oh, I need him now.

She even managed to spare a thought for the blonde stewardess, who was having to brave her way through this ordeal without a man to cling to at all.

There was the clunk of the landing-gear descending, the slowly changing note of the engines, then the bumps, irregular and awkward, of the plane hitting the runway.

The engines roared into reverse. The pressure of the plane's deceleration seemed so powerful that she could have touched it in the air. Then slowly the roar faded, and the plane was taxiing to a standstill.

'Not the smoothest of landings,' Jake said quietly. 'I guess the pilot's pretty jumpy, too.'

Claire raised her head and looked at him. His face was very close to hers.

'I guess he is.'

'One more bad moment behind us.'

'True.' She managed a fragile smile.

'Want a good one, for a change?'

Her eyes connected with his. There was something still and reassuring in his gaze. It was as steady as his arms, which were wrapped around her, with not a trace of his own nervousness apparent.

'I guess I do.'

His lips came down on hers gently, but confidently, sure of their welcome this time, sure of her response. He wasn't demanding passion from her—and she couldn't have given it—just giving and taking that basic human closeness that makes every disaster seem a little more bearable.

The erratic thought came into Claire's head: if I do have to die, there are worse moments than this for it to happen.

Then the kiss ended, and she wasn't dead, wasn't even changed; she was just Claire Middleditch, except that for some barely understandable reason she happened to be sitting in Jake Eagleton's arms, in a hijacked aircraft on a runway in Tunis.

She pulled away from him, suddenly embarrassed by the naked need she had shown.

'What now?'

'Probably nothing much. We wait.'

They waited.

CHAPTER FIVE

THE annoying thing about a hijack, like almost any newsworthy incident, was that by being there you found out much less than you would learn watching coverage on the television.

Claire and Jake agreed this, wearily, in the long hours that spanned the remainder of the day. They knew that in the plane's cockpit, only yards from where they sat, the hijackers were negotiating by radio with the authorities. But they couldn't see the hijackers, couldn't hear the conversations. Only slowly, as the evening drew on, did they even learn what demands the hijackers were making.

Those were very much as Jake had guessed they would be. The hijackers wanted a statement of the FLNG's case published in various major newspapers; they wanted a dozen political prisoners freed from gaol; naturally, they wanted an assured getaway. Some of these demands might conceivably be met, Jake assured Claire, but she knew for herself that this was by no means certain.

Something else was being discussed over the radio, too. The hijackers were almost certainly making threats. They were probably setting deadlines for a response; perhaps they were threatening to start killing people if the deadlines were not met.

Claire and Jake didn't talk about this. Instead, they talked about each other.

Jake was a good storyteller. By evening, Claire felt she would know any member of his family if she passed them on the street: his mother, plumpish and cheerful, his tall, thoughtful schoolteacher father, his younger brother Giles, his sister Rosemary. He told her all about his childhood on the Durham coast, about the rock-pools and the beaches and the fishing-boats; about his school, his Sunday school, outings with his family, holidays with relatives down south. And she told him about her childhood, too; about her mother and father, and the quiet, restful, pleasing life they had lived in Winterton.

Claire liked the sound of Jake's family. Roots were important to her, and it pleased her to think that he came from a secure, happy family, just as she did. But, at the same time, she had always longed to belong to a household that was rowdier and more cheerful than her own, to have brothers and sisters, and she rather envied Jake his tales of escapades along the seashore with Giles and their friends.

They didn't talk about Philip, or about anything in their present lives. This wasn't part of real life, Claire thought to herself; it didn't have anything to do with Philip or with photo-journalism assignments or with the foundations of hotels. It was like a strange niche in time, that found a couple of hundred people stranded together in a capsule. She and Jake weren't trying to build the basis of a lasting relationship, they were just talking to pass the time.

And slowly it did pass. Two of the stewardesses appeared, and under the watchful eye of the hijackers they nervously distributed breakfast. Coffee at last, tinned grapefruit, a bread roll, the whole plastic paraphernalia of an airborne meal. How welcome it was.

'Should we save some of the food?' Claire asked Jake, secretly hoping that he would say no. There wasn't enough to completely quell her hunger as it was.

Jake shook his head. 'Eat it all. If all the passengers do, then we'll all be desperate for another meal at about the same time. Somehow we'll get one. Trust me.'

She did trust him, so she did as he advised.

The hijackers even allowed the passengers to visit the lavatories, though they had to wait their turn, and to leave the cubicle door ajar. Not that Claire would have wished to close it: there was a powerful stench in the little cubicle, and it was suffocating even with the door open.

She read another two chapters of Frank Jackson's book. Jake swapped *The Terror* with a four-day-old French newspaper, and settled down to do the crossword. They both talked to the plump Frenchman, whose name was Jean-Pierre, and to the family behind, whose small sons seemed thrilled by the whole incident.

The blonde stewardess—Marie to them by now— brought out her first-aid kit, and attended to the man who had tried to bring down the dark hijacker. He was all right, she assured them—only a cut on the head. She worked through all the passengers row by row, checking to see if they had any medical conditions.

'Do you think there's any chance of passengers being freed?' Jake asked her.

'It's hard to say,' Marie replied. 'There are two pregnant ladies further along the plane, and a couple of babies. One man's a diabetic, and another in his seventies has already had a couple of heart attacks. The pilot's negotiating to see if they at least can be let off. As for the rest of us . . .'

'We sit it out,' Jake said cheerfully.

'I guess we do.'

They sat it out. Claire began to ache, and her legs felt cramped. She longed to go for a brisk walk, but it would be hours more before she could even walk the few yards to the lavatories again. It was hot. She felt dirty and sweaty and frustrated.

'If only we knew what was happening,' she complained to Jake, for the umpteenth time. She peered out of the porthole yet again, but there was no sign of life out on the tarmac.

'Probably nothing,' he said. 'Authorities conferring worldwide, governments making contingency plans.'

'But how long? How long?'

'Days more, most likely. Want to play noughts and crosses?'

She turned from the porthole to look at him. It was no easier for him than it was for her, she thought. If he could manage to keep not only calm but reasonably cheerful too, she ought to be able to do the same.

'I warn you, I'm a demon noughts and crosses player.'

'So am I. Got any paper? A diary or something?'

More hours passed. Claire won twenty-seven games of noughts and crosses, Jake won thirty-five. Outside the plane the sun began to go down, but it was still very, very hot. She was hungry again, very hungry. She resisted the temptation to say this to Jake. He was doubtless hungry too.

'Do you know how to play Mastermind?' she asked him.

'I'm not sure. Remind me.'

Jake proved to be good at Mastermind: his mind worked more logically than hers. He won twenty games and she won eleven, with a bit of nudging from him. They started to play hangman.

'It'll be sunset in a few minutes,' Jean-Pierre said.

Jake glanced across the aisle with a disapproving expression. That surprised Claire; it struck her as a harmless remark.

'So it will,' he said. 'But the lights in the plane will probably stay on all night.'

'Oh, dear, will they?' groaned Claire. 'So we won't be able to sleep.'

'We will when we get tired enough. Come on, let's play another game. I've thought of a great word, you'll never get this one.'

He sketched a row of ten dashes in the margin of the French newspaper. It wasn't easy playing hangman. So many words seemed to have a connection with hijackings, disasters, discomfort, food...

'E,' Claire said.

'Two Es.' He wrote them in.

Sunset. It suddenly came to Claire. The hijackers must have set a deadline; quite probably they had chosen sunset.

No wonder Jake had been annoyed with Jean-Pierre: he didn't want her to think about deadlines, and what might happen after them.

'Come on, honey. Pick a letter,' Jake urged.

'Sorry, I was miles away. R.'

'No Rs. I told you, you'll never get this one.'

'X, then.'

'No Xs.'

'Boy, you sure play a hard game of hangman! Let me see. S.'

'Curse it, there is one!'

Claire tried hard to catch on to the enthusiasm with which Jake was playing the silly game. It was hard for him too, she knew. She almost shouted out the letters, at top speed. 'T?'

'No Ts.'

'J?'

'No Js.'

'C?'

'One C.'

'N?'

'One N.'

'Got it! Unnecessary.'

'Claire, Claire! There's an E at the end! And no Rs.'

'Curses. Er—U.'

'No Us.' Jake drew in the head of his matchstick man.

'This one's a real pig. Let me think.'

She only had half a second to think, when her attention was drawn away by a commotion at the front of the plane. Instinctively, both she and Jake looked up. Another man had emerged from the cockpit, a thickset man with a heavy black beard whom neither of them had seen before. He was arguing with the hijacker who had been stationed at the bulkhead, in a low, hissing voice which was rapidly growing louder.

'Can you hear?' Claire asked. 'Can you speak the language?'

'No and no. Give me another letter.'

'But, Jake, it might mean...'

'It might mean anything. And whatever it means you can't do anything, you can't change anything, and it's best not to think about it. So pick another letter.'

'But, Jake, we can't just...'

'We can and we must. Nothing's happened, Claire. Don't think about it. Play the game.'

Claire stared at him. She had never heard such a harsh note in his voice before, never before seen so clearly the steel beneath his easy-going manner. He meant it, meant every word of it, and he wasn't going to be persuaded by any argument she used against him.

'You want me to find some other way to distract you?' he asked, in a low voice.

He might kiss her again. But she didn't want that, not when half her mind would be on the hijackers arguing about she dared not think what, only a little way away from them.

'No need,' she said in an unsteady voice. 'I'll keep playing.' She stared blindly at the margin of the paper with its little row of letters and dashes. 'Let's try I.'

'Bother, that'll give it to you! Three Is.'

'Three! Hey, I really have got it. Indecisive.'

'One to your side. Want me to choose another word, or...?'

Claire sensed movement behind them. The dark hijacker had left his position, and was walking down the aisle. She watched for a second as he approached the two men arguing at the front of the plane. Jake touched her shoulder.

'No, I'll choose one. Let's think. Dash-dash-dash...eight letters.'

They played on. Jake gently but firmly persisted every time Claire's attention wandered. The argument was still going on. The passengers were all sitting; their conversations had fallen off; there was a heavy air of tension in the cabin.

'Elephant,' Jake said, with disgusting speed. 'My turn. Nine letters.'

But the argument had ended, and the hijackers were moving again. Claire couldn't keep her attention away from the scene at the front of the cabin. The dark hijacker stalked back down the aisle, the sweat shining on his swarthy face. Behind him, the bearded man also set off down the aisle. He stopped next to a row of seats perhaps ten in front of them, and appeared to be ordering a man out of his seat.

Jake took her hand. 'For what it's worth,' he said in a low voice, 'this is almost certainly a bluff.'

Perhaps it was, but that didn't keep away the chilly hand that was squeezing her heart once more, or the shivers that were pulsing down her limbs. She couldn't reply. Down the aisle, the bearded hijacker was brandishing his gun, and the man he had picked on was shouting abuse at him in a harsh American accent.

'No! No!' A woman began to scream hysterically as the hijacker manhandled the American out of his seat, and dragged him towards the front of the plane.

The dark hijacker was shouting now, as if he was trying to drown out the woman's screams. And Jake determinedly folded Claire back into his arms.

'You go in for praying much?' he whispered.

'Not generally.'

'Well, I guess this is a good moment to start.'

It was, but what did one pray at such moments? The only prayer Claire could remember was 'Our Father'. She began to recite that to herself, silently, over and over again.

The screaming was going on and on. Her senses were all on edge. She was waiting for other noises, gunshots or something similar, but no other noises came, just screaming and screaming and screaming.

'It was a bluff,' Jake whispered.

Claire lifted her head. 'Is it over?'

'No. But if he'd meant to go through with it, he'd have done it straight away. He's human too, he wouldn't spin it out if he really meant to do it. He's just working on making us scared.'

'Well, he's sure succeeding!'

'Sure is.' Jake squeezed her again.

Claire more than half believed him but, though her mind told her he was probably right, she couldn't altogether push away the terror. The screaming subsided into a choking sob. One of the babies started to yell again. They sat there, holding each other tight, for what seemed like a long time. Then there were new shouts, shouts from the hijacker in his loud, guttural voice, and the two of them looked up, almost in the same motion.

The American was stumbling back along the aisle, his wrists bound behind him, with the hijacker following and hitting out at him with his pistol. It was a vicious and terrifying scene, but the man was still alive. He sagged into his empty seat, and the hijacker aimed a kick at his leg, and then turned and strode back towards the cockpit.

There was silence in the plane for a long moment, and then everyone started to talk at once.

'As bad moments go . . .' said Claire.

'That was a record-breaker.'

'I don't know if I could stand many like that.'

'There won't be.' Jake was rapidly regaining his usual confidence. 'You know, that's the turning-point. If he couldn't go through with it this time, he won't be able to go through with it next time. And he knows it; that's why he was so angry with himself. He'll maybe not even try again.'

'So what happens now?'

'I'm not sure. If there had been a killing the troops might have stormed the plane, but I don't reckon they'll do that now. We wait, they negotiate. Eventually we'll be set free. It'll probably be slow and undramatic from now on in.'

'Days,' Claire said.

'Hell, you'd rather have days of boredom than more moments like that, wouldn't you?'

'Much rather,' she agreed.

'So would I.'

'Maybe we ought to ration our paper.'

'There's still plenty left. We can always use the margins of Frank Jackson.'

'That would be a pity.'

'The whole thing's a pity.'

They were neither of them in a mood to resume the game, and there didn't seem to be any urgency to do so, now that the drama was past. They sat for some time, talking occasionally about nothing much. It grew dark outside on the tarmac, though three or four powerful floodlights were trained on the plane, and inside it all the lights were blazing. Jake was right, Claire thought; the hijackers would never allow them to be turned off.

'Do you think we'll eat again tonight?'

'I think there's a chance now, but we shouldn't bank on it.'

'Is there water in the lavatories?'

'None at all.'

She was so thirsty. Maybe no food till morning, or even later. It was a miserable prospect.

Marie and another stewardess reappeared: Marie to attend to the American who had been picked out and dumped back, and the other woman to check the babies.

'I think they'll release the sick passengers,' Jake murmured. 'The hijackers must be hungry, too. They'll maybe do a deal, swap food for hostages.'

'Gosh, I hope you're right.'

He was. Half an hour later, steps had been drawn up, a little band of babies and mothers, pregnant women and sick, elderly passengers had been released, and a van had driven up to just below the plane. While two of the hijackers stood on guard, guns drawn, the stewardesses went to fetch piles of plastic dishes.

It was a typical airline dinner, some sort of nameless stew, a little cake with a cherry, and a hard roll and butter, but it tasted delicious to Claire. And, better still, there was a large glass of orange squash with it.

'Save some of the drink,' Jake advised her. Then a few minutes later he said. 'I think they're refuelling. I can't see much, but I can smell it.'

Claire peered out of the porthole and sniffed. She couldn't see much either, but, above the lingering aroma of the food and the stench of sick and sweat and overflowing lavatories, she could just make out the smell of petrol.

'Will we be moving on?'

'Maybe, but not certainly. It might just be a general preparation the hijackers negotiated. I think you should try to sleep. I'll wake you if anything happens.'

Claire put her head back against the headrest of her seat, and closed her eyes. It didn't feel right. The bright lights shone through her eyelids distractingly. She could hear the low murmur of conversations, and the shouts and laughter of the two little boys just behind her. She could smell the fusty, stale smell of the aeroplane.

She lay there with her eyes closed for some time. Then she opened them again slowly, and glanced at Jake. He was writing in his diary.

'Jake?'

'Uh-huh.'

'Can I ask you a silly question?'

'Ask away.' He smiled, lazily. 'Mind, I might not answer.'

'When you said—when you said I didn't love Philip, you told me it was my clothes that made you think that.'

'Yeah.'

'What did you mean?'

'You really want to know?'

'I think so.' Claire felt uneasy now. The casual comment had felt like a criticism, and she wasn't sure that she was in a frame of mind to take further criticism from Jake.

'It's not just your clothes. It's your hair, your make-up, the whole way you walk, even.'

'That tells you I don't love Philip,' she murmured.

'That tells me you don't love and feel loved. Hell, I don't know this guy Philip, it's nothing personal against him.'

But it's something personal against me, Claire thought edgily. She suddenly felt that it was a mistake to have asked him. She didn't know what to say next, so she didn't say anything.

Jake let them sit in silence for a few minutes, then he said in a low, gentle voice, 'You know, you're a very beautiful woman, Claire.'

'Very beautiful?' She sat up, angrily. 'Oh, come on! You don't have to give me that sort of nonsense!'

'And you don't believe it. That's what I meant.'

'But I—I mean, I'm so tall and . . .'

'So are lots of top models, but they don't make a fault out of it, they stand tall and walk proudly. They call attention to themselves; you don't. They wear clothes that fit really well. I don't mean skin-tight, I don't mean overtly sexy, but I mean confident clothes, clothes that tell you they're proud of their bodies. While you, you hide away in baggy trousers and floppy shirts and—well, look at you now.'

Claire didn't particularly want to look at herself just then, not after twelve hours or so on a hijacked aircraft without a wash or change of clothes, but she couldn't help glancing down at the loose-fitting beige slacks and shirt she had put on for her journey.

'I thought these were nice clothes,' she said, a little grouchily.

'They are in their way. The colour's OK, the fit isn't terrible, but there's nothing about them, about you, that makes one think: this woman's aware of her body, she's telling the world she's pleased with herself. Your hair, too. It's lovely hair, long and thick, and a beautiful honey colour—and instead of letting it hang loose, or coiling it up well, you scrape it back into that terrible ponytail.'

'It's practical,' Claire muttered.

'So are lots of hairstyles.'

Claire thought. It was true, she supposed, that Philip never showed much interest in her appearance. He never commented on her clothes, never made suggestions about how she might do her hair. But she hadn't thought that a sign of his lack of love; it had just seemed a basic trait of his personality. He took a bare minimum of interest in his own appearance, too.

She tried to explain this to Jake, in an awkward, tentative kind of way.

Jake listened, then he said gently, 'Look, I'm not telling you to switch to warpaint and plunging necklines. That's just not you, Claire, and I can see it never would be. But what kind of lover is this guy, if he isn't interested in your body? If he doesn't make you feel pleased with it? If he doesn't love you in a way that makes you feel warm and sensuous, that makes you want to splash on perfume and dress to turn him on?

'You weren't giving me any kind of come-on back at the hotel, and I guessed from your attitude that there was someone in your life. But the signals you gave out then, the signals you give out now, don't say, here's a fulfilled woman who has already found her man, who gets from him everything she needs; they say to me, here's a woman who's unawakened, who doesn't know her own sensuality.'

That's true, thought Claire. How true. Philip had never been a lover in the sense that she knew Jake was talking about. He was more of a family friend, one who had naturally gravitated to her side because she was close to his age, and they were both unattached. He had often kissed her, but their physical intimacy had never gone beyond that. He certainly wasn't the sort of man who would give her presents of silk stockings or frilly undies, who would make her feel frivolous and feminine and desirable.

Perhaps that would change a little when—if—she married him. Perhaps she did come across to an observant man like Jake as the inexperienced virgin she really was. She wouldn't stay an inexperienced virgin after her marriage. But she knew instinctively that even then Philip would be unlikely to unleash vast reserves of sensuality from within her. She believed she would come to feel fulfilled in a staid, married sort of way, but she was conscious that if she married Philip she would never think of herself as a sexy woman.

She had never thought of herself like that. Even 'sensual' wasn't a word that she had ever thought applied to her. It was a quality other women possessed.

Did Jake really see that potential in her? she thought wonderingly.

She turned and glanced at him. He had it, she thought; he was a sensuous man. He wasn't a fashion-plate, not a male-model type at all, but he had the sort of physical awareness that he was talking about. He was confident in his own attractiveness, aware of his own body, and everything about him—his choice of clothes, the cut of his hair, his stance—proclaimed that to the world.

A flood of unnerving images swept through her brain. She couldn't help imagining what it would be like to be the lover of a man like Jake, a man who wanted her to wear her hair loose and dress in satin underclothes and smother herself in expensive perfume. A man who adored her body, and made love to every inch of it with obsessive, concentrated admiration. She couldn't help thinking of how she might flower in the sunlight of his loving attention. While with Philip it would be a life of cotton nightdresses and cocoa at bedtime, a life not of growing, but of growing older.

'You see what I mean?' Jake asked gently.

'In a way.'

'Then do something for me. Let down your hair.'

It was a statement, not a request, put softly but firmly. And there wasn't anything overtly sexual about it, but Claire felt herself blushing, all the same, under Jake's tightly focused gaze.

'Sounds dumb, doesn't it?' he said cheerfully. 'Take off your glasses, Miss Smith. But I really want you to do it, Claire.'

'I'll feel like an idiot.'

'I don't think you're an idiot. I think you're a beautiful woman.'

Strangely enough, she believed him this time. And she didn't stop him when his hands reached out and gently pulled the elastic fastening off her hair. He ran his fingers through it, spreading it across her shoulders.

'Got a comb?'

'In my bag.' She fumbled at her feet, dragged the bag out from where she had pushed it under the seat in front, and retrieved a plastic comb.

'Thanks.' Claire had expected him to leave her to comb her own hair, but instead he took the comb from her and began to comb it himself. He did it slowly and carefully, concentrating, smoothing the strands with his fingers.

It was oddly soothing, sitting there in the aeroplane while Jake combed her hair. She wasn't conscious at all of the other passengers, or of the hijackers, slumped in weary concentration over their weapons. Nobody seemed to be paying them any attention, and it felt almost as if the two of them were quite alone.

But they weren't, thought Claire, and in a way that added to her sense of security. Jake might kiss her again, she thought, but she knew that however much she relaxed her guard they weren't in a situation where he could take things between them any further.

Finally he set the comb down, slipped his fingers through her hair one last time, and said softly, 'That's better.'

'OK,' Claire murmured.

'You look like Sleeping Beauty. And now you can go to sleep.'

The gentle pressure of his hand on her shoulder drew her down against him. His arm wrapped round her, her head nestled into the hollow of his shoulder.

'Comfy?'

'Mmm.' The lights were still blazing, the danger was still lurking, but now she felt perfectly at peace, totally at ease in Jake's arms.

The last thing she was conscious of before the world faded away was the soft brush of Jake's lips across her forehead and his voice whispering, 'Sleep well.' And then she slept.

CHAPTER SIX

THE first thing Claire thought when she woke up was that they were moving. She sat up, awkwardly, nudging Jake's restraining arm out of the way, and knuckling the sleep out of her eyes.

'Yes, we took off about ten minutes ago.'

'And I slept through it! Why didn't you wake me?'

'Why? You've seen aeroplanes take off before. You don't even like take-offs. What would I wake you for?'

That was unarguable. Claire shook her head to try to clear some of the fug that filled it.

They were in the air again. It was the proper place for an airliner filled with passengers, but it wasn't reassuring, not with the hijackers on board. She felt suddenly, acutely claustrophobic.

'Look at it this way,' Jake said, as if he were following her thoughts. 'Nobody's going to storm the plane while we're in the air. Nobody's going to be threatened. There are no deadlines. We're safer here than we were on the ground.'

'Yes, but nobody's going to set us free, either.'

'That's true,' he agreed.

'So where are we going?'

'I'm not sure. We're flying east, that's all I can tell. The pilot hasn't told us anything this time.'

'East,' Claire echoed.

'Libya. Egypt. Maybe Cyprus or Syria. It's hard to say where we're going.'

'Will it make much difference?'

Jake grinned. 'Well, the further we go, the longer it'll be before we get any breakfast.'

'Thanks,' Claire said sarcastically.

'Drink your orange,' he advised her.

Astonishingly, half of her drink from the previous evening was still on the little tray in front of her. She reached for it, and was about to take a big gulp when she remembered how long it might be before she had another drink, and settled for sipping it slowly.

'What's the situation for the——'

'Lavatories? There's a new system now, you put up your hand. I warn you, it's pretty disgusting back there.'

'I can imagine.'

In fact, the state of the cubicles dwarfed even the most lurid stretches of her imagination, and it was all she could manage not to be sick before she bolted out again. Thank goodness their seats were not right at the back of the plane, she thought, as she made her way back to Jake.

'When we get out of this plane,' he said, as she slid past him and sat down again, 'they'll take us to a big hotel. An American hotel, with luck, a Marriott or a Hilton or something, with tiled bathrooms and showers that work at high pressure and free sachets of shampoo. And I'm going to pull off every stitch of clothing and get under that shower and stand there and stand there and stand there.'

'Mmm. Mind, you'll be in trouble if you don't get your suitcase back first. Then you'll have to put your dirty clothes back on afterwards.'

'No sweat. I'll call room service, and breakfast in the buff.'

Claire laughed. She could just imagine Jake lolling back and devouring American-style English muffins on a big American-style hotel bed.

'However,' he went on, 'I do have a spare shirt and underpants and socks with me. I always carry a change of clothes in my hand luggage. The worst time ever, it was three days before my suitcase caught up with me, and I learned my lesson after that.'

'Lucky you,' Claire said enviously, conscious of the sweaty and disgusting state of her own attire.

'You're welcome to the shirt if you'd like it. No comments about baggy clothes, I promise. I'm not sure the underpants or the socks would be much use to you.'

That was a really generous offer, Claire thought. But it didn't seem fair, taking Jake's clean clothes and leaving him in his dirty ones. Anyway, she didn't like the thought of standing in that revolting lavatory with the door half-ajar and the dark terrorist peering through the crack while she swapped shirts.

'Thanks,' she said, 'but I'll leave it until tomorrow.'

'Well, the offer's open.' Jake sat back. 'At least it's cooler up here.'

It was, but the air in the cabin was stale and fetid in spite of all that the air-conditioning could do. How much longer will it be? Claire wondered. How long until we all break under the strain, or fall sick in these unhygienic conditions? She could guess the answer. The hijackers' demands had clearly been refused, and they hadn't gone through with their threat to kill a passenger. The authorities would wait until they broke, now, and it was hardly likely that those fanatical, fit men would be the first on the plane to crack.

And then what? The storming that Jake, clearly, had half expected at Tunis? Or perhaps the hijackers, in despair, would find a way of blowing up the plane, and everyone on board with it?

'Want a cheerful scenario?' Jake asked.

Claire glanced at him. 'The shower's fine,' she said, 'but it's the bit between now and then that's causing me problems.'

'Try this one for size. Hijackers know that the longer their hold-up goes on, the less likely it becomes that the authorities will give in to their demands. International opinion hardens, and nobody will be panicked any more into giving in to them. But the authorities know, too, that these are desperate men. The minute the first freedom fighter pulled out his gun, they'd virtually thrown away their futures.'

'So there's nothing for them to lose by sticking it out.'

'Not so. Many men can handle staring death in the face for a few minutes, but doing it for days and days on end—that wears down the toughest guy pretty soon. The longer you think about pulling the trigger on yourself, the more attractive a long prison sentence comes to sound.'

'Does it?' Claire asked dubiously.

'It does. These guys haven't killed anyone, remember. They've brought their cause some publicity. If they fall into the hands of a reasonably sympathetic government that promises not to extradite them, they can reckon to be free again before they've too many grey hairs.'

'So they'd negotiate...'

'In the end, they'll negotiate simply for that, for the hope of a fairly short sentence, and the promise that they'll be saved from deportation back home. That's a way many hijacks end.'

'Do they?'

'That, often. Sometimes the hijackers just throw in the towel. Sometimes the authorities set up a charade of giving them their freedom. They hand over a getaway car, for instance, but they wire up the fuel gauge to full and then all but empty the tank so the car will run out of petrol and they can surround it half a mile down the road.'

'You know it all.'

'So do the authorities. So do the hijackers, most likely.'

'So it's a game of bluff.'

'Usually it is. And the authorities have already called these guys' bluff once. They did that when they let the deadline pass yesterday.'

'It sounds . . . possible.'

'That's what it is. Hey, I laid my hands on an English *Times* while you were asleep, and the crossword's only half finished.'

'I'm lousy at crosswords.'

'No, you're not. You just haven't learned all the tricks yet. Let me teach you.'

Jake spread out the crumpled newspaper on his knee. This one too, Claire noticed, had little pencil games scrawled all down its margins. Her hair flopped forwards when she leaned over to look more closely at it, and she pushed it back, self-consciously, with one hand. She half thought of tying it back again, but it was pleasing, the thought that she had untied it for Jake.

'A good half of these clues are anagrams,' Jake was saying. 'So the first thing's to count the letters, and work out which words make up the anagram. Let's take this one, eighteen across, for instance . . .'

He was wrong, Claire had decided within ten minutes; she would never make a crossword solver. Even when she knew the answers, most of them didn't make any kind of sense to her. But all the same she enjoyed bending over the paper with him, their heads close together, and watching him incisively explain his reasoning, and set down the answers in his firm, neat handwriting.

She looked appallingly disreputable herself, she knew from her fleeting glimpse in the mirror, and Jake had a hefty dark stubble prickling across his chin, but in spite of that, in spite of their unwashed state, it was still pleasant to be close to him.

Finally the plane began its descent, through a cloudless sky, towards an anonymous-looking coastline and a mass of houses that made up a city by the sea.

'Recognise it?' Claire asked.

Jake frowned as he gazed through the window. 'There are half a dozen places it might be, but I can't say for certain. Won't make much difference to us.'

'If you say so, sir.'

'Maybe we'll tell from the breakfast,' Jake said cheerfully.

But there wasn't any breakfast. The plane stopped, they looked out of the portholes at a collection of ambulances and army trucks much like those they had left behind, and then nothing happened. After a while they stopped expecting anything to, and returned to their familiar time-passing activities.

The air in the cabin was fuggy now. Some passengers had persisted in smoking almost throughout, and a thick blanket of stale cigarette smoke seemed to be creeping down over their faces. Several people dashed to the lavatories, complaining of feeling sick. The children in the row behind, so well-behaved earlier, fought and argued and jumped on the seats, and then complained of empty tummies and sore mouths.

Marie began to work her way down the aisle again, making a new list of those who were suffering most under the strain.

We won't be on it, thought Claire. She tried to imagine what the ordeal would have been like if she hadn't had

Jake next to her, but some stranger she couldn't stand, or a foreigner she couldn't talk to. Would she feel half as strong as she did now? She was anxious to escape, more than anxious, but she didn't feel as if she was in imminent danger of breaking down; and Jake himself seemed as calm and confident as ever.

They somehow managed to pass another hour. Two hours. It was ten-thirty by Claire's watch—more than twenty-four hours since they had boarded the plane. And now they and the plane were heaven-knew-where, and she was probably further away from home than when she had started!

Certainly home seemed further away from her. It was Jake whom she clung to, Jake whom she trusted to see her through. Except when she had been telling him about them, she had barely thought about her parents or Philip since the ordeal began.

That thought, now, brought her a pang of guilt. They must surely know by now from the newspapers or the television that she was a passenger on the hijacked plane. Perhaps they were all sitting around the television right then, watching pictures of it. Perhaps they knew where she was, even though she didn't. That was a peculiar thought.

She looked across at Jake. He was talking to Jean-Pierre again, desultorily, leaning back in his seat with his legs stretched as far as they would go in front of him. He had discarded his jacket and tie hours before. His shirt was unbuttoned at the neck, and the sleeves were rolled up to just below the elbow. He looked almost piratical, with the stubble on his chin and the dark shadows under his eyes. But this was a good pirate, Claire thought, a pirate she could trust. She couldn't imagine leaving the plane and saying goodbye to him forever.

Not that there was any sign of their leaving. The hijackers changed places sometimes, argued among themselves in their incomprehensible language, made the occasional barely convincing show of fierceness, but there was no sign that things were approaching a crisis.

Steps were rolled up. It was the familiar trade-off again: half a dozen sick passengers for a meal. The atmosphere in the cabin was so nauseating now that Claire found she could scarcely eat it, although she had thought herself starving. Nobody seemed to be showing the enthusiasm they had shown over the previous day's dinner.

Even Jake pushed his tray away after a dozen mouthfuls, and said dully, 'I guess I could afford to lose a pound or two.'

'I guess you already have.'

'Reckon so.'

The stewardesses too were worn out, and the trays sat there for almost an hour before they came to clear them away. Another long pause. And then the intercom crackled—a noise they had not heard for so long that they had almost forgotten it was there.

'Ladies and gentlemen, this is your pilot again. I have some news for you.'

Claire sat up and concentrated. Underneath the weariness, there seemed to be real excitement in the pilot's voice.

'You'll know that the freedom fighters on board this plane have been negotiating with the authorities ever since they first took charge yesterday. And now, thank goodness, they've succeeded in coming to an agreement.'

The cheer was so loud that the rest of the pilot's speech was drowned by it. Then calm slowly restored itself, and the pilot went on to explain the details. The hijackers had agreed to give themselves up as soon as a declaration they had worded had been broadcast on a dozen major television networks. They had been negotiating the arrangements for leaving the plane safely and, as Jake had predicted, they had been promised a local trial, and assured that they would not face deportation.

Claire turned and looked at Jake. He was already looking at her.

'Honey,' he said quietly, 'I reckon we're safe.'

'I reckon we are.'

'Hey!' He reached out, and pulled her back into his arms. He hugged her so tightly that her ribs ached, and she hugged him back, just as hard.

'Mustn't cheer,' he said, more soberly. 'The hijackers won't like that.'

Claire couldn't honestly make herself care what the hijackers thought. But they weren't off the plane yet, and she realised that what Jake had said made sense, as usual. Though the hijackers had come to terms with the authorities, they had still failed. They had lost their gamble; they were weary, disappointed and fundamentally desperate men.

Indeed, the dark man at the back of the plane was waving his gun now, and shouting at some of the passengers who were laughing and hugging each other in front of him. A moment later the pilot's voice came on again.

'Keep calm, please, ladies and gentlemen. Please. I must urge you to keep calm. Now the freedom fighters want to address you once more, and when they've finished I hope I'll be in a position to announce the arrangements for leaving the plane.'

There was a groan, quickly suppressed, from a few of the passengers, then a few crackles, and the guttural voice of the bearded hijacker came over the address system.

Claire looked out of the porthole as he spoke. There was movement on the tarmac now. She could see more ambulances drawing up, and there were crowds of people milling about outside one of the buildings, behind a rope barrier. It's true, she tried to tell herself. It's almost over.

The hijacker droned on and on. It was frustrating to face yet another delay, but the passengers were too relieved to have the prospect of freedom to be really impatient. Finally his propaganda speech came to a close, and the pilot returned to the microphone to tell them about the departure arrangements.

'The hijackers insist on choosing a hostage each,' he explained. 'They'll leave the plane with their hostages, armed, and when they get to the terminal buildings they'll give themselves up to the local police. Then the police will tell us when the rest of the passengers are free to leave.'

Claire shivered. Hostages! For four unlucky passengers, there would be yet another ordeal to bear.

And already the bearded hijacker and two companions were making their way down the aisle, looking over the passengers. She gave a bare glance behind her, and saw the dark hijacker moving, too.

'Don't look,' Jake hissed in an undertone.

She looked down at the floor. But it was too late, the dark hijacker had seen her glance, and he stopped in the aisle next to Jake, brandishing his gun and waving at Claire.

'He's choosing you, *mademoiselle*,' Jean-Pierre said helpfully, in a thick French accent.

'No,' Jake said harshly. 'No. Claire, you're not to go. I'll go with him.' He turned to the hijacker, and tried to explain in mime that he was offering to act as the hostage.

But the hijacker shook his head, and waved his gun again in Claire's direction.

Claire took a deep breath. 'I'll do it, Jake. It's only for a few minutes, then we'll all be free.'

'Claire, you mustn't. It's too dangerous. Let me do it.'

'You can't, Jake. He's chosen me.'

Claire set her hands on the armrests of her chair, and pushed herself to her feet. Her legs felt unsteady under her. She couldn't help thinking about the gun. Would he touch her with it? Would he hold it to her head?

'Claire, please! No! Don't do it! He'll take me, if I insist.'

Jake was standing too. He set his hands on her shoulders, and tried to press her back into her seat. Claire reached out shakily, and put out her hands to push him away.

'It's OK,' she said. 'I'll see you in a minute. OK?'

At the front of the plane, the other three hostages were already standing in the aisle with the hijackers. Marie was one of them, Claire saw. The other two were male passengers she didn't recognise. The bearded man shouted to the dark hijacker, telling him to hurry along, presumably.

On impulse, Claire reached up and kissed Jake quickly on the mouth. Then she slid past him, and nodded to the hijacker, who took her upper arm in a firm grip.

They edged down the plane. One by one, they edged down the steps. The hijacker was holding Claire's arm twisted behind her back now, and she could feel the cold

metal of the gun at her temple. She was almost too terrified to move, and she stumbled once when he pushed
her forward.

Then they were on the tarmac, and she was being
shoved forwards, all the time with the gun at her head.
It was less than fifty yards to the terminal building, but
it felt like a hundred miles. Then, at last, policemen in
an unfamiliar dark uniform were surrounding them, and
she felt the light pressure of the gun ease away.

She didn't know any more, because she fainted clean
into a policeman's arms.

'Claire! Claire! Darling, can you hear me?'

The voice seemed to be coming from a long way away.
A familiar voice, comfortingly familiar, except that for
some reason the person speaking sounded so upset, dis-
traught almost. Claire thought this confusedly, through
a strange, thick fog that seemed to swirl around her.

'Claire! Open your eyes, please, Claire!'

But they were open, she thought irritably. Then she
blinked to prove to herself that they were open, and
found that they weren't, after all. Slowly, painfully, she
eased her lids apart.

It was all right, everything had to be all right, because
there was Jake, and his arm was around her and his face
was close to hers. She let out a little sigh, and closed
her eyes again.

'OK, darling. Take it gently. It's all right now. I'm
here with you.'

I know that, Claire thought mistily. Then she felt as
if she didn't, quite, and she reached out a hand, blindly,
and found it connecting with a firm male body.

The body moved, and somehow she found her hand wrapping around it, and two strong arms cocooning her in a strong, warm, immensely comforting embrace.

A moment later she did open her eyes, though she couldn't see much more than a close-up of a patch of Jake's shirt. She breathed in and smelled him, faintly spicy and faintly sweaty, and then she moved her head a little, and he caught her movement, and eased his hold so that he could look down at her.

'We're safe,' she murmured.

'We're safe. We're at the airport, and all the hijackers have been captured, and there's nothing to worry about.'

Claire nodded.

'My brave girl,' Jake whispered, and he bent down and let his lips just brush across hers.

Claire willed him to do it again, but he didn't. Instead he drew gently away from her, and said, more firmly, 'When you're feeling up to it, we'll try and get out of here. The authorities have fixed all the passengers up with hotels, but we have to run the gauntlet of the Press before we can get out and to safety.'

She took another deep breath. Her limbs were beginning to feel as if they belonged to her again. She put a hand behind her, and pushed herself upright. She had been lying on a bench, she discovered, in a small room that was practically full of people.

'What did I . . . where . . .'

'You fainted,' Jake said gently. 'Only for a few minutes, after the hijacker brought you over to the terminal. The police brought you in here, and then just now they let the rest of us off the plane, and I came to find you. We're in a departure lounge, and the Press are being kept back on the other side of immigration control.'

'I think I see,' Claire said faintly.

'Do you think you can stand up now?'

'I'll try.'

She could, just about, so long as Jake supported her. Around her, she saw many of the other seated passengers getting to their feet. 'Oh,' she said weakly, 'were they waiting for me?'

'A couple of passengers have already gone off in ambulances,' Jake said, reassuring her that she hadn't been in the worst state possible. 'And Marie passed out, too; she's only just come round. Now I think the rest of us will be able to get moving.'

Some of the passengers, seeing Claire get up, had already made for the entrance, and soon, with a posse of policemen guarding them, they had made their way through the corridors and checkpoints of the airport, and out into a brightly lit foyer.

Flash! Flash! A dozen cameras were trained on the crocodile of passengers. Voices shouted from all directions. Claire made out some questions in English, though most were in foreign languages. What was it like? What did the hijackers say? Did they threaten you? Were you very frightened? What was the worst thing about it all?

What stupid questions, she thought confusedly. She was glad that Jake was there, his strong arm holding her up and protecting her from the worst of the onslaught.

As they came closer, some of the journalists and photographers seemed to recognise her. 'That's the girl hostage,' one of them yelled, and others called out to ask her questions.

'Don't answer them,' Jake murmured in her ear. 'There's no need to say anything.'

Claire couldn't have said anything if she'd wanted to, she was too confused by the lights and the noise and the clamour. All she wanted was to lie down again and go to sleep. She clung to Jake, and somehow they managed to edge their way past the microphones and cameras, and out to a waiting bus.

The next period passed by in a blur. They were driving through the outskirts of a totally unfamiliar Middle Eastern town, with police horns blaring on all sides of them. They were being ushered through the foyer of a very large and plush hotel, past more banks of pushy pressmen. There was a lift, a corridor, and then a smiling man was opening a door, and ushering her and Jake into a bedroom.

It was such an immense relief when the man made his way out again, bowing and smiling, and closed the door behind him, that she didn't think of anything more than falling into Jake's arms, and feeling him hold her tight.

For a long time neither of them spoke. Then Jake raised his head and said unsteadily, 'Hell, I shouldn't have let this happen.'

'What happen?' Claire asked, confused.

'Them putting us in a room together. Look, I'd better phone down and ask them to find me a different room.'

He let her go, abruptly, and strode over to the phone that sat on a chest of drawers between two expanses of bed. Claire collapsed on to the nearest bed, bewildered.

Jake picked up the phone.

'Jake,' she said weakly.

He looked up. There was an odd, strained expression on his face.

'Claire, are you all right?'

'Jake, don't leave me. Please, please don't leave me!'

It was slowly sinking in that that was what he intended, to leave her alone in the room and go somewhere else. It was a thought that struck her with panic, and her voice rose almost to a shriek. Jake hurriedly moved over to her, and set his hands on her shoulders.

'Claire. Darling, please!'

'You mustn't go, Jake, you mustn't!'

'Look, I can get someone to come and stay with you, if you like. One of the women on the plane, maybe. Marie, or...'

'I don't need anyone else. I need you!'

There was a short, charged silence. Then Jake said gruffly, 'Hell, I'm not leaving you. I couldn't leave you now.'

'Don't. Please don't go,' Claire kept whispering, as his arms crept round her again.

'It's OK, darling. It's OK. I'm here, I'm staying here.'

She could feel her heart beating wildly, feel his hammering in counterpoint to it. She could feel the ragged warmth of his breath on her cheek, and the only thought in her head was that she had to have him there, had to keep him with her.

Finally the beating settled into a steadier rhythm, and she was able to ease her grip on him without the panic setting back in.

'You want that shower now?' Jake asked unsteadily.

'I think I just want to sleep.'

'Me, too.' He got up, and went across to the window. He drew the curtains against the blazing sun outside. Then he came back to the bed and wrapped his arms round her again, and they lay down together, and promptly both fell asleep.

CHAPTER SEVEN

CLAIRE woke to darkness, and a sensation of warmth. She was lying with her body pressed tight against a man's body, and she knew, even before her mind began to work properly, that it was Jake. She surfaced to the sensation of his hands roving over her, possessing, claiming, arousing, the heat of his breath, the murmur of his voice, so low that she could barely hear it, repeating her name under his breath.

'Jake,' she whispered back. 'Jake.'

His hands seemed to scald her skin where they touched her. He pushed up her shirt and ran them across the bare skin of her midriff. She turned so that she was still closer to him, and her own hands reached out for him.

His mouth traced the line of her jaw, tantalisingly, and then tracked a path down the column of her neck, and nuzzled at the neck of her shirt. He brought his fingers round to unfasten the buttons, and she lay back unprotesting and let him remove it. Her eyes were used to the dark now, and she could see the shape of him, solid and black against the less intense darkness of the hotel room.

The thought passed through her mind—Jake is making love to me. It was all unfamiliar and strange, but at the same time it seemed natural and inevitable and right that they should be here together. She was fully awake now, and she knew what was happening, what was going to happen, and she thought with utter certainty—this is what I want.

She reached out and began to unfasten the buttons of his shirt. Her hand sneaked inside when she was half-way through, and caressed his bare chest. She could feel the hair that curled across it, silky smooth, feel the taut muscles in his side. The sensation seemed to travel down her arm and into her body, and gather into a tight bud of longing somewhere deep inside her.

Jake shrugged off his shirt and gently unfastened her bra. Then he lowered himself down against her so that their bodies touched all along their length. Her nipples felt almost raw, they were so alive to the sensation of his touch. She moved her body under him, slowly, wondering at the power of the feelings that were gathering force inside her, and his mouth bent down to claim hers.

His kiss was as sweet as she remembered it, firm and confident, but there was a force to it now, a possessiveness, that was even more powerful than it had been when he had kissed her on the path leading to the guest house. It was as rawly male as the rough rasp of the stubble on his chin. I'm his woman, Claire thought, and she opened her lips to welcome his sweet invasion of her mouth, brought her tongue into play to tease and excite and welcome him with an instinctive expertise she had never known she possessed.

The movements of his body, his tongue, the surge of blood through her veins, all seemed to speed into an insistent rhythm. Philip's kisses had never grabbed her as this feeling did. They had always been pleasant, but there had been nothing urgent about them, no feeling of abandonment, always a cool certainty that she could take them or leave them without particular concern. This was different, this was elemental. The urgency of the need in her was so strong that it was almost a desperation. She clasped at Jake, grabbed at the tensed muscles of his shoulders, as if her insides had turned to a vacuum and she had, simply had, to fill it.

Jake seemed to feel it too, because there was nothing left now of the leisurely manner in which he had begun their lovemaking. He almost yanked at her slacks as he pulled them down and off her, and when he sat up to unzip his own trousers it was with the same grim urgency. Claire watched him, tense with impatience to feel his body back against hers, and at the same time a little shy of helping him.

All this was new to her, totally new, both the experience of an all-but-naked male body against her own, and the flood of sensation that threatened to overwhelm her. She had never been aware before of this emptiness within her, this space that cried out to be filled by her man. The sweet agony of his mouth, his tongue, tracing a trail of fire across her abdomen and down to her thighs, the hard jut of his body against hers, the confident urgency of his fingers, seeking out her body and making it known, in a way that was as unfamiliar to her as her body was to him: all of this was strange and incredible and unbelievably glorious.

She opened her mouth, half intending to tell him that she wasn't used to this, she had never done it before, she needed help. But she didn't voice the words. She wasn't afraid that he might stop, she knew instinctively that they had both passed well beyond the point when they might have turned back. It simply didn't seem true any more that she didn't know what to do. Her body knew it. It had this extraordinary knowledge that she had never sensed before, had never even dreamed she possessed: this primitive, urgent awareness of what it needed, and how to set about getting it.

When he bent to rip away her panties, she found herself pulling his off in the same motion, her nervousness forgotten. Her legs, her arms, her mouth—everything parted to welcome his joining with her in that ultimate union of man and woman.

There was just a moment when he was surging against her and he seemed to hesitate, to be caught in his rhythm. Then her body opened to him, and the little sensation that was more of a surprise than a pain was gone, and she was being carried deeper, deeper into a bottomless cavern of ecstatic fulfilment.

The ache that focused within her, the knot of pressure, dissolved, and the relief seemed to flood outwards in waves of sheer delight. The pleasure pulsed stronger and faster, faster, and then Jake was panting, and gave a hoarse cry, and the sensation was fading, and the two of them collapsed in an exhausted, sweating heap together on the bed.

For a long time they lay there together, not moving, with no sound but the rasp of their breathing as it slowly returned to a steady rhythm. Then Jake sat up, and propped himself on one elbow as he looked down at her.

'Now we really do need a shower,' he said softly.

Claire smiled. 'What on earth time is it?'

'Heaven knows. Some time after midnight and before dawn. If we're quiet, we won't wake anyone.'

He reached out for her, and his hand wrapped round her wrist. Limply, she let him pull her to a sitting position. Then he reached out to switch on the bedside-lamp, and turned round again to meet her look, and smile.

His look, his touch, was full of reassurance. Claire had been scared for a moment that he would wreck their mood by bringing up the subject of her inexperience, that he would feel obliged to apologise for making love to her at a time when she had been so vulnerable. But she didn't want his apologies, didn't want to be made to feel guilty for giving herself to him. She needed to be reassured that she had done the right, the natural, the only thing possible in the circumstances, and his look told her all of that.

'Come on,' he whispered.

She slithered over to edge of the bed, and set her feet cautiously on the floor. They held her. She did feel different. It was all strange, this odd sensation of heavy fulfilment that she was wrapped in, this feeling that she had been stretched to her limits and then released again into total relaxation. But she was still Claire, and her legs still obeyed her when she tried to set one in front of the other and walk to the en-suite bathroom.

Was it a Hilton, or a Marriott? she wondered, wryly amused, as she glanced around at the expanse of white tiles and the thick piles of fluffy towels. Whatever it was, it was just the kind of American luxury hotel, luxury bathroom, that Jake had dreamed of out loud in the plane. And when he switched on the shower the water cascaded out in a fast, scalding torrent which was again precisely what he had ordered.

He regulated the temperature carefully, then reached out for her, and gently drew her under the shower with him.

It was an odd sensation, standing naked with Jake under the powerful jet of water. But she didn't feel embarrassed at her nudity, even in the bright light of the bathroom, or about Jake's hands gently soaping the grime and sweat off her. It was bliss, absolutely as blissful as she had dreamed it would be in the long, mucky, dirty hours of the hijack, to be standing there, feeling the water drive away all the painful memories, and wash her mind as clean as her body.

They stood there for a long time, not talking, with the hiss of the shower echoing in their ears and the water pattering down on them. The last bubbles dissolved, and the water ran hot and clear down the curves of their bodies and dripped off and drained away.

Slowly Claire's mind began to work again. She tossed back the sodden, heavy mass of her hair, and brushed the water out of her eyes. Jake was smiling when she looked at him. And he continued to smile, faintly, as her eyes surveyed his naked body.

She had seen him wearing nothing but shorts at the hotel when she had first knocked on his door, what seemed like a lifetime before, so the sheer muscular power of him didn't come as a surprise to her. But she hadn't liked to let her eyes linger then. He hadn't been her man then. Now he was. Now she could feast her senses on every inch of him, let this new knowledge of her sight blend with all that she remembered of his touch, his smell, and make him seem totally hers. Her mate, everything she had ever wanted her man to be.

Even the faint stirrings of his rearousal, spurred by the unconscious sensuousness of her look, didn't embarrass her. When she brought her eyes back to his face, it was to catch the happy laughter of his eyes, and to be caught up again in his embrace, in the joyous knowledge that there were no threats now, no deadlines, and they had all the time in the world to take pleasure in each other.

They swayed in and out of the fierce jet of water, letting the force of it add an erotic charge to the lingering sensuousness of their kiss. Finally Jake pulled her, dizzy and laughing, out of the tub, grabbed a couple of towels from the pile, and half carried her back to the nearest bed, where he threw down the towel, one-handedly spread it across the coverlet, and eased her down on top of it.

The urgency was less this time, the desperation gone. There was time to savour him, to linger over every touch, every sensation. He left the bedside-light on, and she could see him clearly in the dim, pinkish light, catch each expression as delight, desire, intense concentration and sheer joy passed across his face.

She wouldn't have believed it possible that her body could feel such desire again, so soon after its first experience. Only half an hour before it had felt as if she was fulfilled so totally that it would last for a lifetime. But under his gentle, expert ministration her senses came back to life, the fire flickered in her again and then began to burn, with a strong flame that was all the more powerful for the underlying knowledge of what it would be like when the explosion followed.

Slowly, absorbedly, they scaled the peaks of ecstasy once more, and then slid down in mutual contentment to the comfortable foothills, lying sated in each other's arms.

'I never dreamed it was like this,' Claire whispered in wonderment.

Jake smiled again. His grey eyes looked almost violet in the soft light of the bedroom, and his face looked softer too, the jutting lines all blurred in his relaxation. 'It isn't always,' he said softly, 'but this is how it should be.'

'This is,' Claire agreed. It all seemed so totally right: Jake himself, each look, each touch, everything was exactly as it should be. Her contentment was so total that there was no room in her mind for guilt or hesitation.

She closed her eyes, as if to recapture in the darkness the perfection of the moment. And slowly the world slipped away, and she slept, deeply and dreamlessly, once more.

They were woken together by the harsh sound of the telephone ringing by the bed. Jake rolled over and reached out to answer it, and Claire groggily let herself surface to wakefulness, to the sun beating through the curtains and the heavy, still air of a hotel room in a hot country.

Her mind finally focused itself, and she turned her concentration to what Jake was saying on the telephone. 'Ten o'clock,' he said, in a voice that told her he was agreeing with a suggestion. 'And it's——' he reached for his watch, next to the telephone, and glanced at it '—eight forty-five now. OK, we'll be down by then.'

'Who was that?' Claire asked, as he set down the receiver.

'An official from the British Embassy. We're to meet him in a conference room at the hotel later this morning, with the other British on board the plane.'

'The British Embassy,' Claire echoed.

'That's right. Seems they want to debrief us and check on what we'll say to the authorities and the Press, before they let the rest of the pack loose on us.'

The rest of the pack. That had an alarming sound to it. Slowly, a crack appeared in the warm cocoon of Claire's contentment. It rapidly widened into a yawning chasm.

The honeymoon was over, almost before it had begun. In an hour it would be back to business: the sordid business of dealing with the authorities, retrieving possessions, testifying against the hijackers and eventually making their way back home.

Except that, unfairly, incomprehensibly, her home wasn't Jake's home. Claire glanced at him, suddenly worried, wondering what he would suggest now, how they would get through the ordeal that lay immediately ahead—and, even more important, what would happen afterwards.

Jake returned her look levelly. 'It won't be so bad,' he said. 'Everyone knows we've all been through a terrifying experience, they won't expect wonders of us. We'll see how you cope with the first meetings, and then if you don't feel up to any more I'll make sure that the Press don't get at you.'

We'll see. That was what she wanted, what she needed to hear—that they would face the ordeal together, side by side, hand in hand. Alone, it would have been too much for her, but with Jake, she told herself, she would be able to do it.

'OK,' she said quietly.

'You can have the first shower. I'll see if I can rustle up some breakfast on room service. Any preferences? Eggs? Orange juice?'

'Yes, orange juice, lots of it. And coffee, too.' She smiled at him, trying to suppress her unease. The words were right, but there was a subtle change in his manner, a distancing that hadn't been there the night before, and that disturbed her.

But she couldn't afford to think about it, not with a difficult morning of interviews ahead. She swung her feet to the floor and padded off to the bathroom.

When she returned a few minutes later, her hair swathed in one big towel and her body wrapped in another, Jake had ordered breakfast and was on the telephone to the hotel reception, trying to find out what had happened to their baggage. He put down the phone a moment later.

'Guess what?' he said with forced cheerfulness. 'It's mucky clothes time. Here, take my clean shirt. No arguments. I'd rather see you clean than feel clean myself.'

'Thanks,' Claire said, without arguing. She surveyed the crumpled heap of her own clothes on the floor without enthusiasm. Jake had done his best, clearly; she knew that if he had had no luck in getting hold of their suitcases she would almost certainly fare no better if she were to try herself.

'They're not even in the hotel yet,' he said, following her thoughts. 'Apparently the police and the airport authorities are insisting on checking through every bag before releasing any of the luggage. It'll be mid-afternoon before we get our hand luggage, and even later before the cases in the hold are sent on.'

'Oh. So we won't be able to fly to...'

'Not till tonight at the earliest, maybe not until tomorrow. Things move slowly in this part of the world, and the police won't let anyone go until they've all the statements they could possibly need. I did ask if we could place international calls, but apparently that's barred too until the police have seen us. Maybe the Embassy people will be able to do something about that.'

International calls. It all came flooding back, the thought of her parents and Philip and all her friends, waiting around in Winterton for news that she was safe. She hadn't even thought of telephoning them the night before. How terribly thoughtless of her!

And what was worse was the realisation that they hadn't seemed to matter, that her mind had been so focused on Jake that she hadn't needed reassurance herself from her family. And now, after the events of the night that had changed everything—her thoughts, her feelings, her body, too—she simply couldn't imagine how she would face them, what she would say to them, how she could explain about all the tremendous changes in her life.

'That worries you?' Jake asked, a little sharply.

Claire busied herself with her hair for a moment, unwrapping the towel and rubbing the damp mass before saying, awkwardly, 'I ought to have thought of it before. They must be ever so worried. I ought to have tried to phone yesterday, I...'

'Claire,' Jake said gently. He crossed over to sit by her on the bed, and put an arm lightly round her shoulders. 'You mustn't blame yourself for anything. You've been under tremendous stress. Even a saint couldn't spare much of a thought for people miles away, in that kind of a situation. You were so exhausted last night, we both were, that it's no wonder you didn't think of your family. They'll understand that, I'm sure.'

'I suppose so.'

'Don't worry about it. You haven't the energy to spare, you're more tired than you realise. Now, you get dressed, and I'll join you as soon as I've showered.'

'That's something,' Claire said, as cheerfully as she could.

Jake got up and padded away, still naked, towards the bathroom. She sat on the bed for a moment once he had gone, then she made herself start moving. She vigorously towelled her hair dry, found her comb, and worked it into some sort of vague order. She put on Jake's clean shirt, which hung loosely about her shoulders, and—with a little shiver of distaste—her own filthy slacks. She looked at her face in the mirror. She looked like a scarecrow. Her hair was drying fast in the heat, and it frizzed a little in tendrils around her face. There were faint circles below her eyes, but she could see, reflected in the mirror, the radiance of a woman who had just discovered love. How extraordinary, she thought. I can see that I look a mess, and yet I've never felt more beautiful.

This was what Jake had meant; she understood it now. This was what he had sensed she had lacked before: this spring of joy that was inside her now, that made her want to float, not walk, that held her proud and tall and happy. This awareness of the body under her clothes, this lingering memory of the pleasure it could give and take. Even her scarecrow clothes didn't diminish the pride. As she brushed her hair she could remember his combing it, the look in his eyes, and she weighed the damp mass of it in her hands, telling herself that it was beautiful, she was beautiful. She would never just haul her hair back, tie it and forget about it again.

She was still looking in the mirror, combing her hair through for a last time, when Jake returned. He walked up behind her, and reached out to sweep the hair from her shoulder and gently kiss the exposed side of her neck.

'Mmm,' Claire murmured.

Jake laughed in her ear. 'I'd better get dressed,' he said. 'Our breakfast will be here in a moment.'

'Mummy! Mummy, is that you?'

The telephone line fizzed and crackled so much that Claire could hardly hear the voice at the other end. But it *was* her mother, she knew that. She could sense the scolding anxiousness, the dissolving worry flooding down the wires towards her.

'Mummy, listen,' she said when the voice faded away. 'I'm all right. Everything's OK, we're safe and well. The

Embassy is arranging flights for us, and I should be home late this evening... Yes, this evening. Ten o'clockish, I think, but I'll try to let you know... Yes, Heathrow... Meet me? If you can manage it.'

There was another loud crackle and a hiss, and then, startlingly clear, the word 'television', and then more crackles. Claire moved the receiver a little away from her ear, and waited for them to die away. Finally the static faded, and she said loudly, 'Mummy? Mummy?'

It was her father's voice this time, booming down the line, louder and more confident than her mother's. 'Claire? Now, do you want me to fly out and join you? I've checked the flights, I could get one in an hour's time.'

'Fly here? Oh, no!'

'But you must be exhausted, and it's a long...'

'Look, I'll be getting to Heathrow about ten. If you just meet me there... OK, Daddy. Yes, of course... Yes, love to everyone... Bye, Daddy.'

She put down the receiver and collapsed, drained, against the wall. They were in the hotel lobby; even luxury hotels in this country, apparently, couldn't arrange international calls direct from the room phones.

Jake uncurled his legs and strode across the foyer to join her.

'Tough?'

She gave him a strained smile. 'It was a bad line, I had to concentrate. But I think I got the message across.'

'That's good. Hey, I think some of the luggage has arrived. Let's go and see if ours is there.'

It was good to have something to do. The scanty details of the conversation were beginning to percolate through her mind, but she wasn't ready to dwell on them yet. She glanced at Jake, his hand on her elbow as he propelled her through the crowd in the foyer. Thank goodness she hadn't had to speak to Philip. She had no idea what she would have said to him.

There, in a corner near the door, were the familiar uniforms of the airline staff, and next to them a jumbled pile of bags and suitcases. Ten minutes later Jake and Claire had emerged, triumphant, with all their baggage.

'Now for some clean clothes,' Jake said.

They went in silence up the lift to their room. It was mid-afternoon; the morning had been taken up by the inevitable bureaucracy, interviews with Embassy officials and local police, aviation authorities and, finally, journalists and television reporters. Many of the media men had focused their attention on Claire and Marie, the two women among the hostages who had been marched at gunpoint from the plane to the terminal building. Jake had tried to shield Claire from the ordeal as much as he could, and she knew that she could never have got through the interviews without the reassuring knowledge that he was right there by her side, holding her hand and squeezing it encouragingly.

Jake unlocked the door to their room, and set down the two heavy cases he was carrying. 'I need a shave,' he announced. 'You want another shower before you change?'

'I think so.'

'Mind if we share the bathroom? I'll keep out of your way.'

Mind? After their intimate shower the night before, would she *mind* if he shaved while she was using the bathroom? It was as clear an indication as he could possibly have given that he was again setting a distance between them.

He hadn't done that during the interviews, Claire thought confusedly. She had needed him then, and he had given her all the support and reassurance she had asked for. But now—now, suddenly, he was acting like a familiar stranger.

'Of course not,' she said stiffly, and bent to unfasten her case.

She tried to concentrate on the motion of showering, of changing, of sorting out her things, and not to be too aware of Jake as he was shaving and washing and getting dressed. But she was conscious of every little awkwardness. He was careful not to touch her at all while she was undressed; he rarely looked in her direction, he barely spoke.

Claire fastened her case and repacked her holdall. She reached for her camera bag, thinking vaguely that she should check through its contents before she left. She undid the buckle and flap—and then froze, horrified.

Every film has been unrolled. Somebody had deliberately pulled them all out of their lightproof cases, and exposed each and every print. The whole lot was ruined.

Jake paused in knotting his tie. He hadn't been looking at her, but he had responded almost instantly to her reaction. Silently, he crossed the room and looked over her shoulder.

'But...' Claire spluttered. 'Jake, who could have done this?'

'I should have warned you,' Jake said in a low voice.

'Warned me?' She glanced around, astonished, 'Jake, you *knew*?'

'No, but I could have guessed. It's the sort of thing the police would do in this part of the world. They've no need of photographic evidence, they don't want it, and so——'

'But my films weren't evidence! They were my work, my assignment!'

'Claire, I'm sorry.'

Sorry. Claire stared at him blankly. Her first big assignment ruined, and her lover was *sorry*.

Jake must have realised how inadequate his response was. Slowly, clumsily, he knelt down by her on the floor of the hotel room, and put his arms round her.

It was the first time she had cried, all through the hijack and its aftermath. And it was ridiculous, somehow, to be crying now over spoilt film, when she had survived so many bigger traumas dry-eyed. But the tears must have been building up inside her, because they came now as a positive torrent. Her body shook with the force of the sobs, her hands clutched at the stiff material of Jake's suit.

Jake held her gently, stroking her hair with one hand and whispering reassurance to her. She sobbed uncontrollably for some time. Then the torrent slowly dried to a trickle, and she raised her head.

'There are some tissues somewhere,' Jake said.

He got up and did a quick search, eventually tracking down a dispenser in the bathroom, and then came back to kneel by her and wipe away the traces of the tears. Gently, very gently, he kissed her on the mouth.

'I'm sorry,' Claire whispered.

'Don't be. You needed to cry.'

'I'd better go and wash my face.'

'I'll be here.'

She lingered in the bathroom for several minutes, splashing cool water on her flushed and swollen face. Finally, when she looked in the mirror, she saw something resembling normality, and she steeled herself to go back into the bedroom.

The films didn't seem to matter, momentarily, though she knew that the disappointment of her ruined assignment would haunt her for years. It was Jake who still filled her thoughts.

He *did* care, she was sure of it. The way he had held her as she cried had been as tender, as full of loving, as any touch the night before. But she knew now, with horrible certainty, what he was going to say that afternoon.

She could postpone the moment, but she couldn't think of any way of cancelling it. It had to come. She took a final deep breath, and pushed open the door.

Jake had been sitting on one of the beds, his knees slightly apart and his head buried in his hands. As she approached he lifted it, though, and gave her a slightly strained smile.

'Better now?'

'A bit.'

'The editor will understand, I'm sure. There's nothing you could have done to prevent it. Even if you'd kept the pictures with you when you left the plane, the police would have taken them at some point. It won't ruin your career. That is, if you still want a career as a photo-journalist.'

Claire wanted to shout, but of course I do! But a more rational part of her mind told her that the certainty she felt right then wasn't to be trusted. Her thoughts, her emotions *were* inevitably off balance in the aftermath of the shattering experience she had been through.

'I guess so,' she said dully.

'Look, it's three-thirty now. We won't be leaving for the airport for almost two more hours. We could go for a walk, perhaps? Or would you rather rest for a while?'

I'd rather make love, Claire thought hopelessly. But she knew that that option was no longer on offer.

'Rest, I think.'

'OK.'

She sat down on the bed that Jake was not already sitting on, and self-consciously slipped off her shoes and lifted her legs on to it. From the corner of her eye, she saw Jake doing the same.

They lay in silence for a long time. Claire closed her eyes, but she couldn't sleep, and she could tell from the soft sound of his breathing that Jake wasn't sleeping either.

Finally Jake said, 'Are you asleep, Claire?'

'No.'

'There's about half an hour before the airport bus goes. Maybe we should make our way down to the lobby.'

'Maybe.' She sat up.

Jake cleared his throat, awkwardly.

'Look, I'm sorry I'm coming on the London flight. I can see it would have been better for us to say goodbye here, but you understand, I have to go and see my family too, and reassure them.'

'Of course,' Claire said dully.

Unexpectedly, he stood up, crossed the short space to the bed where she had been lying, sat down by her, and took her hand.

'I don't want you to blame yourself for what happened last night, Claire, and I'm not going to apologise for it either. But we both know that it happened while we were under stress, in unusual circumstances. I don't want it to change anything between you and what's-his-name, Philip.'

Claire glanced at him sharply. He wasn't looking at her, his eyes were focused on his knees.

'But it has!' she almost shouted. 'Jake, you can't imagine I'd go back to...'

'Of course you will,' Jake said, steadily and firmly. 'Claire, things are going to look very different once you're back home. And when you get back to your family and Philip, I'm sure you'll realise that this was just something that happened in the shock of the moment. They'll understand that, I'm sure they will, and you will too, when you have a chance to think about it more rationally.'

But I don't love Philip! Claire wanted to protest. I know now that I never have, not in the way I loved you last night. You saw that, Jake, you told me so, back at the village.

I love you, Jake Eagleton. She thought it so powerfully that it was hard to be certain she hadn't accidentally said the words out loud.

But he had never said them to her, a little voice in her head broke in. Even in the heat of their passion, he had never told her that he loved her.

In fact, all along he had made it abundantly clear to her that he was not offering her a long-term future. Travel alone, that was Jake's motto. He wasn't a man for marriage or for commitment, he had told her so right at the start.

She couldn't find it in her to regret a single moment of their lovemaking. It had seemed so right, so completely inevitable. It had been so wonderful. But it came to her now that Jake must be feeling very differently. He too had been under stress, he too had let it happen in the heat of the moment, but without knowing, as Claire had known, that she was a virgin giving herself to a man for the very first time. And now, however graceful he tried to be about the situation, he must be suffering from a ghastly combination of guilt and embarrassment.

He doesn't love me, she thought. And now he must be terrified that I'm going to take his rejection badly, that I'm going to weep and plead with him to stay with me.

No, she wouldn't. She wasn't a cry-baby, never had been, and she had already subjected him to one outburst. She would just have to tell herself that he was right, that in the cold light of Winterton what had seemed so natural and inevitable under the hot sun would come to seem no more than a strange aberration. Perhaps when she got back she really would be overjoyed to see Philip. Who knew, perhaps Philip himself would one day make love to her as Jake had done the night before.

She should have said something, she knew, something gracious and generous. But that was too much to ask of herself; the words simply wouldn't come. In the end she just pulled her hand away and stood up, saying in a harsh, edgy voice, 'Let's get going, then.'

Jake stood up too. For a moment he blocked her way to the door; for a moment his eyes touched hers, for what felt like the first time in a lifetime.

'You're a very beautiful woman, Claire,' he said quietly. 'And I'll never forget you, never.'

'I'll never forget you either, Jake,' she managed to say. And I only hope, her heart whispered, that you don't realise how painfully true that will be.

They barely spoke on the way back to the airport, or on the long flight to London. Claire dozed for most of the journey. At Heathrow Jake helped her retrieve her luggage, and walked with her out to the departure lounge.

It was all happening again: the flash-bulbs, the micro-phones, the reporters shouting for interviews. Claire peered past them, helplessly. And there, to her immense relief, was the tall, familiar figure of her father.

'Daddy!' she shouted. Somehow she managed to cover the next few yards, and then both her parents were hugging her.

When they set her free she looked around for Jake. But he was nowhere to be seen.

CHAPTER EIGHT

'I THINK the pink definitely suits you best, Julie. Don't you, miss?' A pause. 'Miss?'

Claire woke up from her daydream with a start. 'Oh, yes, definitely the pink. Much more flattering with your colouring.'

'Maybe you're right,' Julie said. 'I'll take it, thanks.' She disappeared back into the changing cubicle.

Meanwhile, her friend gazed idly at Claire. 'Hey,' she said a moment later, 'you are, aren't you? The girl in the hijack?'

'Well, actually, I...'

'I knew it! I recognised you from the telly. Never forget a face once I've seen it. Julie! Guess what, this is the girl who was in that airline hijack! Golly, I bet you were terrified! What was it like, when that hijacker picked you out...?'

Claire suppressed a sigh, and resigned herself to politely telling her story. Again. It was her first day back at the boutique, and already five people had walked in and asked her about the hijack—either seeking her out on purpose or, like this pair, recognising her face from all the publicity there had been.

She had to be polite to them all, because it was her job, but oh, how ghastly it was being reminded again and again about the whole incident, when what she needed was to put it all behind her, to get Jake out of her mind, and to settle down to the steady routine of her daily life. And she had been so looking forward to getting back to work, too, to escape from the oppressive concern of her parents in the long, empty days after her return.

Automatically, she finished folding the pink blouse and slipped it into one of the boutique's green and grey carrier bags. She processed Julie's credit card, smiled and spoke her thanks, and saw the two customers out of the shop.

Four-thirty. Another hour, and it would be time to go home. Philip had wanted to take her out to dinner that evening, but her parents had protested that she would be too tired after her first day back at work, and would need a quiet evening at home and an early night. Claire hadn't objected because she hadn't felt ready to face him yet, and still had to sort out the confused mass of her own feelings. Anyway, her parents had been right, she thought now: she felt exhausted.

'The palace never likes to name the day too precisely, but our understanding is that the baby should be born around the twelfth of January.'

'Well, isn't that nice?' said Claire's mother, standing up and crossing over to change channels at the end of the nine o'clock news. 'Some really pleasant news for once. There's nothing quite like a royal baby, is there?'

'Nothing,' Claire croaked, in a voice that she hoped didn't sound as odd to her mother as it sounded to her. 'Excuse me a minute, Mummy.'

'Don't be too long, dear. The film will be starting as soon as the adverts are finished.'

'I don't think I particularly want to watch it.'

'Oh, well, please yourself.' Her mother settled back down into her armchair, and took a sip of her mid-evening cup of tea.

Claire groped her way to the stairs, and up them. She pushed open her bedroom door. Somehow she found the strength to close it again, and then she slumped down on to her bed.

A baby. She simply hadn't thought about babies before, but the pictures on the television of the radiant princess had suddenly sent the thought slamming into her head. The princess's baby would be born in January. And if she were pregnant herself, when would hers be born?

No, she couldn't be. It simply wasn't possible. It wasn't the sort of thing that could happen to her, Claire Middleditch. Never, not even in her worst nightmares, had she ever before imagined herself becoming an unmarried mother.

But the thought had come now, and it wouldn't go away. She couldn't make it go away until she had given herself time to think it over, and space to be realistic about the possibilities.

There was no denying it, she had made love, and the thought of precautions simply hadn't entered her head in the hotel bedroom. Nor had Jake thought of this basic necessity, she realised now. They had both been exhausted, and swept away on the tide of their passion; the risk of pregnancy hadn't been any more real to them than the guilt they would feel afterwards.

But it was real to her now, and as a doctor's daughter she knew all about the likelihood of its happening. It didn't make any difference, she knew, that it had been her very first time. Indeed, it had been the time of the month when she would have been at her most fertile. There had to be a very strong possibility that the worst would have happened.

Her mind wouldn't work straight. She had to get her diary out of her handbag in order to work it out. At the very best it would be another week before she knew for sure. The shock might have upset her normal regular cycle, so it could be longer: ten days, perhaps more.

Jake's baby, she thought, with a sudden sense of wonder. I might be carrying Jake's baby.

But it wasn't a wonderful discovery, she knew, it was a terrible one. Jake had made it absolutely clear that he didn't intend to see her again. She didn't even have his address, and she hadn't given him hers. If she really was pregnant, she wouldn't have any way of contacting him to tell him so. And what could she tell him, anyway? He had said he had no intention of marrying her or anyone else. He would be concerned and sympathetic, perhaps, but she wasn't at all sure that he would offer to marry her under those circumstances, or even that she would want him to. He might even suggest that she have an abortion. That thought was too awful to bear.

She had to know, and as soon as possible. A pregnancy test, that was the thing. She couldn't go to the chemist in Winterton, it would be all round the town if she did, so she would have to find an excuse to go to London. Then, when she did know, if it turned out to be true, she would have to think about what to tell her parents, and Philip, and...

The plans and possibilities spiralled in her head. She tried to make herself be realistic and practical, but it just didn't seem real that she, Claire, should be in this situation. She reached down and felt her stomach. She didn't feel any different from usual; she didn't feel pregnant. But perhaps girls in her situation didn't, she thought.

'Claire!' her mother called from the bottom of the stairs. 'Phone call!'

Claire jumped up, with that odd anticipation she felt every time the phone went—the hope that it might be Jake. Then, as always, came the knowledge that it couldn't possibly be. She knew who it was even before she picked up the receiver. It was Philip.

'Good day at work?' he asked briskly.

'Yes. Tiring.'

'But you'll be all right by Wednesday, won't you?'

'Wednesday? Why, did I...did we...?'

'Dinner, then. Eight o'clock. I'll need to phone and book a table tonight, because the restaurant gets busy, Giles told me.'

'Which restaurant?' Claire asked, confused.

'It's called the Catalan. I thought we'd have a special evening out to celebrate your coming back home safely.'

'Philip, I...' Claire began, and then her voice tailed off. She wanted somehow to ask for time, to warn Philip that everything was different, but she couldn't think of what to tell him, or the words to put it in.

'I'll pick you up about a quarter to eight, then. And I'll maybe drop round tomorrow, if I'm not too busy.'

'I'm still a little...'

'Look after yourself,' Philip said. 'See you then. Bye, darling.'

'Bye,' Claire said automatically. She heard the click of Philip ringing off, but she stood there for a moment, staring at the receiver and wondering what she should tell him.

Claire still hadn't worked out what to say when Philip appeared promptly at a quarter to eight on Wednesday evening. She had only seen him briefly since the hijacking, and she had been hoping that the sight of him would somehow clarify her feelings. But it didn't, she just felt dead inside, and rather tired and still very worried. A part of her felt that she would do best to break off her relationship with Philip straight away, before she even knew whether she was pregnant; but another part whispered that she was still off balance after the drama of the hijacking, and that this wasn't the time to make such important decisions. That was what her parents would have said if only she had felt able to confide in them, she was sure, and she was hoping that she would be able to ease her way through the date with Philip without coming to a firm decision about her still very uncertain future.

Philip didn't seem to notice her low mood. He was obviously determined for them to enjoy a special evening out. The restaurant he had chosen proved to be a country house a few miles away, very plush, and much more expensive than the curry-houses and steak-houses that he normally took her to. He talked all through the meal, about his work, his friends, and all he had been doing since Claire went on her trip. Then, when the waiter had poured their coffee, he leaned towards Claire, across the restaurant table, and said in a lower, more intimate voice, 'I think you've guessed what I'm going to say now.'

Did he know? Claire thought suddenly. How could he? She didn't even know herself yet if she was pregnant or not. A moment's more thought made it clear to her that Philip must be thinking along quite different lines. He wasn't a man prone to self-doubt; it would never have entered his head that she might have fallen in love with another man, let alone given full expression to that love.

'Philip,' she said awkwardly, 'I'm afraid I'm not good company tonight. I'm still getting over the hijack, and...'

'Nonsense,' Philip said briskly. 'You've been excellent company. You always are, Claire. And, though the hijack was a terrible experience, in a way I feel that it's helped us, because it's brought home to us how much we really do matter to each other.'

Has it? Claire asked herself. She looked intently at Philip. His face was clearly lit by the candle on their table. It was pleasant and familiar, and to look at him was comforting in a general sort of way. But he wasn't Jake, and though she had known Philip for a long time, and Jake for only a few days, she couldn't help feeling desolate at the knowledge that the man who was with her was not the man she loved.

Jake had said that he didn't want their relationship to change things between her and Philip, but that wasn't something that you could decide by sheer will-power, Claire thought to herself. It *had* changed things, and she couldn't help feeling that, even if she proved not to be pregnant, she would never again be able to persuade herself that she loved Philip Anderson.

'It's made me think, Philip,' she said.

'And me, too,' Philip agreed. He reached across the table and took her hand. 'I know we said we'd take it slowly, Claire, and wait until Christmas before we formally announced our engagement. But now that this has happened, I don't think we need to wait any longer.'

Oh, no! Claire went cold inside. She should have seen it coming, she realised now, and yet it was all so very, very far from how she had been thinking and feeling herself that she simply hadn't anticipated it. She should have worked much harder to divert him from this; it was the last thing she wanted. But it was too late now, Philip was steaming solidly ahead like an ocean liner.

'Picture it all, Claire. Imagine you and me together in our first house. Imagine us having our first baby, how thrilled your parents will be. I can just see our children growing up in Winterton. Picture us together as old fogeys, sitting watching the television side by side.' He gave a gentle laugh; this was his idea of a joke.

Claire could picture it. That wasn't difficult, since Philip was portraying just the kind of life that her parents lived. It wasn't the life she had ever imagined for herself, though. Even when she had more or less taken it for granted that she would marry Philip one day, she had always dreamed of herself carrying on as a photo-journalist. Watching the television side by side, that wasn't what she had wanted at all! She had wanted drama, excitement, the wide world at her feet.

And look where one short taste of the wide world had got her, she thought sadly. With her first big assignment in ruins, and the threat of an unplanned pregnancy hanging over her, she couldn't make herself believe any more that she would succeed in creating for herself a glamorous career in the media. It was all too likely that she would end up as an unmarried mother, existing as best she could in a tiny flat and bringing up her baby alone.

Set against that grim picture, there was something gently appealing about the prospect that Philip had put before her. The futures she saw for herself were all full of terror and loneliness, while Philip's future sounded stolid and contented. She felt like a tightrope walker who wobbled on the high wire, and saw the safety net beckoning from below. Look too long at the net, and it became impossible to keep your balance and carry on walking the wire.

But she couldn't accept him, she thought, with an odd mixture of relief and sadness. It wouldn't be right at all to get engaged to Philip while she might be carrying Jake's child. She would have to say no. The time for waiting and thinking was over, she had to tell him her decision now.

'Philip...' she began tentatively.

Philip didn't seem to hear her. 'Claire,' he said. He pulled her hand towards him, across the tablecloth. 'I'm asking you to marry me.'

'Philip, I can't.'

'I hope you like the ring,' Philip went on. 'I bought it at Jones's, and Mr Jones assures me he'll change it if you're not perfectly happy with it. You're going to be wearing it for a long time, so...'

He freed one hand and reached down to fumble in his pocket. Claire managed to seize the opportunity to say again, this time in a much firmer voice, 'Philip, I can't accept you. I'm sorry.'

Philip froze in mid-motion, one hand in his pocket, one on the tablecloth.

'Can't?' he echoed, coming slowly back to life. 'Don't be ridiculous, Claire. Of course you're going to marry me. We've been agreed on that for months.'

It was true, they had. But now everything had changed. Claire wanted to tell him that, but at the same time she didn't want to hurt him, and she didn't know exactly what to say. That she had met a man, loved him for a little while, and now didn't expect to see him ever again? It was the truth, and in her heart it felt like a very good reason for saying no to Philip. But would Philip think it a good reason? It would hurt him, she knew. But he wouldn't understand it. He would most likely argue, as Jake had done, that she had been off balance, still was off balance, and shouldn't take such a big decision at such a time.

'The hijacking, Philip,' she said in a low, shaking voice. 'It gave me a terrible shock. I know there's no danger now, but I don't feel that I'm over it yet. It's not the right time for me to make this kind of a decision.'

'The right time?' Philip frowned. A queer mixture of emotions seemed to chase each other across his face, as if he hadn't yet worked out whether he was upset, or angry, or would manage to be patient and understanding about Claire's unexpected response. 'Decision?' he echoed. 'I hadn't thought of it as a decision, Claire. It's something we've been moving steadily towards for a long time.'

'In a way we have, I know. But it means making a much deeper commitment, and at the moment I simply don't feel I'm in the right frame of mind to make it.'

Philip took a deep breath. Apparently he had decided to be calm and reasonable.

'Look, Claire, nothing will happen straight away. I'm not asking you to marry me tomorrow. Naturally there'll be an engagement period, perhaps a long engagement. You'll carry on working in the boutique, and you and your mother will plan the wedding, and—well, I thought maybe next summer would be the right sort of time...'

Next summer. By next summer, Claire thought to herself, her and Jake's child might be sitting up and smiling at her. That thought wasn't real. None of it seemed real: this picture that Philip held in front of her, the prospect of having Jake's baby, the knowledge that he had gone out of her life as suddenly as he had come into it. None of it made any sense to her heart.

'Philip, I'm sorry,' she said again. She pulled her hand away from his, and realised with vague surprise that it was trembling.

'You'd like some time,' Philip said in a stony voice.

Was that what she wanted? All she wanted just then was to be away from the restaurant, away from this painful scene, and on her own. She nodded numbly.

'Then I'll take you home.'

Philip paid the alarmingly large bill. He dutifully pulled back her chair, retrieved her linen jacket from the waiter and held it while she slipped in her arms. His hand accidentally brushed hers as he moved to usher her towards the door. It seemed as coolly impersonal as any doctor's touch; there was no element of flirtation in it, no sensuality.

They walked side by side to Philip's car, neatly parked in the car park outside. How tall he was, Claire thought. Six foot three, a good four or even five inches taller than Jake. But he didn't make her want to walk tall, as Jake had; with him she felt herself slouching. She hadn't felt beautiful since that morning in the hotel. The day after she had arrived home she had tied back her hair in its familiar ponytail.

They drove in silence back to her parents' house. Philip drew his car up outside and switched off the ignition.

'Naturally I'm disappointed, Claire,' he said in a quiet voice, 'but on reflection I think you may be right. All the medical authorities are agreed that the mental effects of shock persist for quite some time after the incident that brings it on. Perhaps this isn't the most appropriate time to celebrate our engagement. Your birthday's next month, isn't it? Maybe we should think of making the announcement then.'

'Maybe,' Claire said.

'I'll come in for a few minutes. Your parents will think it odd if I don't.'

They thought it odd anyway, Claire realised as soon as the two of them came into the living-room. From the eager glances that her parents turned towards them, she realised that they had been told, or had guessed for themselves, that Philip had been planning to propose to her. Philip shook his head sideways, in a silent warning, and immediately her mother rallied round as if Claire was an invalid, to be handled with kid gloves.

She felt acutely guilty, as she perched on the sofa, living up as best she could to Philip's tale of her crashing headache that had brought them home early, and listening to Philip heartily discussing the evening's television news stories with her father. None of them understood, and she couldn't explain to any of them how and why her feelings had changed. Philip thought—they all seemed to think—that they would change back again once she was completely over the shock of the hijack. But Claire couldn't believe that it would be so.

The next week passed for Claire in a state of barely veiled panic. The little boutique was rarely busy, and there were sometimes long stretches when no customers came in. Mrs James left her in charge alone, and she had nothing to do but think.

None of her thoughts were cheerful. She tried not to think about Jake, but he crept into them all too often. She thought long and hard about what she would do if she really was pregnant. She thought about what she still had to tell Philip. He had told her father on the day after their dinner that they had agreed to announce their engagement on her birthday. It wasn't what they had agreed at all, as Claire had understood it, but she had come to feel that it might be as well if she took advantage of the month's grace that it had given her. Or, at least, of as much of it as she needed—because, if she found that she really was pregnant, she felt that she would have to break the news to Philip, and end their relationship immediately.

But she didn't yet know for certain. On her afternoon off she caught the train to London, and in a large chemist's she bought herself a pregnancy-testing kit. She hid it at the bottom of a drawer in her bedroom when she came home.

She was late already. The instructions said you could use the kit even if you were only twenty-four hours late, but she kept on postponing it from day to day, hoping to be reprieved.

And she was. She hardly dared to believe the first signs, but soon there was no doubt. She was definitely not pregnant.

It was an immense relief, an overwhelming relief. Mixed with the relief was a tiny bit of sadness, too, because she knew that now she would never have a baby by Jake Eagleton. But she felt it wouldn't have been fair to give birth to a fatherless child, so she did her utmost to tell herself that it was definitely for the best. There hadn't been a happy picture in her mind of herself and Jake with their baby. That picture had died with her photographs of the little resort, in a hotel room half a continent away.

CHAPTER NINE

JOHN WILKINS, editor of the *Sunday Tribune*'s colour supplement, leaned forwards over his messy, paper-strewn desk, his cigarette dropping ash over a pile of cuttings.

'You think I'm angry, Claire?'

Claire flushed. 'I reckon you're pretty annoyed,' she said bravely.

'You're damn right. I'm livid!' He waved his cigarette in the air and stood up abruptly. He took a couple of paces and then turned around. 'But not with you.'

'Not with...'

'I'm livid at those damn hijackers, *and* at the idiot policemen who wrecked your pictures. But it's not your fault, kid. Even an experienced reporter wouldn't have fared any better in that kind of situation.'

'It's kind of you to say so.'

'I'm not in this business to be kind. I aim to be fair, that's all.' He paced some more, and took another drag on the cigarette.

'You want to go back?' he asked abruptly.

'And retake the pictures?' Claire couldn't help shivering at the thought of getting on a plane once more. She thought for a moment, then she said, 'I know I accepted the commission, and I still have my notes for the story and everything. But I honestly don't know that I could face it at the moment.'

'Maybe not. It's a lot to ask.' John Wilkins paused. He dropped what remained of the cigarette and ground

it out on the floor under his foot. 'You want me to run
your story with another guy's pictures?'

'I'd understand, if you wanted to do that. I mean, it's
cost you a lot of...'

'Hell, we waste commissions all the time, there's no
sweat about that. You written it up yet?'

'Not yet. I'm afraid I...'

'You written up anything about the hijack?'

'The hijack? No, of course not.'

'Of course not,' John Wilkins mimicked, in a cruelly
accurate voice. 'You really want to be a journalist, kid?'

Did she? If she had really wanted to be a journalist,
Claire thought uneasily, she would have gritted her teeth
and got on the next plane back, to take more pictures
to replace the ruined ones. If she had really wanted to
be a journalist, she would have started writing a piece
about the hijack as soon as she got off the plane—while
she was still on it, even—and by now she would have
sold it to every newspaper in the country.

Her very own exclusive, the one time when she had
been where all the action was, and the thought of writing
it up hadn't even occurred to her! From the way she had
been acting, it was reasonable enough for John Wilkins
to assume that she didn't really want to be a journalist.
He would have been hard pushed, she admitted to
herself, to make himself think anything else.

'To be honest, I'm not...'

'To be honest, you're still shaken, aren't you?'

'A little.'

'Then let me give you some advice, kid. You go back
home. You take a rest for a couple more weeks. Then
you phone me again, and I'll fix you a new assignment.'

'That's very generous of you, really it is. But I'm
honestly not sure that I deserve it.'

'You do.' John Wilkins sat down again, and lit another cigarette. 'Claire, you ain't never going to make a war reporter, not in a million years. You'd never make a foreign news correspondent. You'd never be fool enough to even try, I can see that. But I still think you've the makings of a damn good photo-journalist specialising in soft features.'

Soft features! It sounded really insulting, but she could see from his face that he didn't mean it to be, so she kept her face still and listened.

'Travel, fashion, celebrity interviews, stories about kids...you know, women's stuff. That's your patch. Don't you listen to anyone who sneers, there's plenty there to keep you going for a lifetime. Now, you take two weeks' vacation, get plenty of rest, have some fun, and then give me a call when you're ready to roll again. OK?'

A little spring of pleasure began to bubble inside Claire. Her patch. It was! she thought with sudden certainty. Not every journalist had to be the sort of hard-bitten hack who could keep one foot in the door of a con-man about to be exposed or a couple of newly bereaved parents. Some journalists wrote and illustrated pleasant articles about fashion and holidays and children. John Wilkins was right, she would never make a war correspondent, but she could, she really could, make a good soft photo-journalist.

And there was no competition, none at all, when it came to choosing between that kind of a life and her job in the boutique. She wanted it!

She stood up, with renewed confidence. 'Thanks a lot,' she said, holding out her hand. 'I'll call you in a fortnight.'

'With some ideas,' John Wilkins said, taking the offered hand and giving it a hard squeeze, and her a flirtatious wink.

'With some ideas,' she agreed, and she walked out of the newspaper offices with her heart leaping for the first time since her return home.

It was an unexpected feeling, because she hadn't thought for a moment that the interview would turn out as it had done. She had known that she had to see the editor and apologise, and try to make some kind of arrangement to terminate her commission. But she had never dreamed that he would give her a second chance. And he had, he had!

She practically skipped down the street and into the tube station. Then she spent the rest of the journey home trying to plan out ideas for features that she might put to the editor when she next phoned him.

It was late afternoon when she finally reached Winterton station. She wasn't expecting Philip to meet her, he would be busy all day. And he was on call that evening, too, so he wasn't likely to drop round at the house. That was a relief to her. She wanted to plan how to tell Philip her news, not least because she had begun to think, on the way home, that this might provide an excuse to break her proposed engagement. Philip wouldn't like the news, she suspected. Perhaps she could provoke him into arguing with her about her career plans, and then she would have a convincing reason to break things off without ever having to explain to him about Jake Eagleton and all that had happened immediately after the hijack.

She wasn't sure that her parents would be thrilled at the news either, but she was eager to share it with somebody, and hopeful that, whatever their misgivings about her chosen career, they would be pleased for her sake.

She retrieved her battered little Mini from the car park and, still in her merry mood, drove the short distance back to her home.

Her mother greeted her in the hallway.

'Had a good day, dear?'

'Very good,' Claire crowed. 'I'll tell you and Daddy all about it this evening.'

'Rightie-oh. Tea, dear?'

'I'll make it.' She hung up her jacket, and floated into the kitchen.

'Oh,' said her mother, in the doorway. 'Claire, I quite forgot for a moment. You're going out this evening.'

Claire finished filling the kettle, then looked up. 'I am?' she asked. 'Funny, I don't remember.'

Her mother moved into the little room. 'I hope it's all right, dear. You weren't here to ask, so I had to make the arrangements for you, and the gentleman sounded so positive that he wanted to see you. I know you don't like to be reminded about all that nasty business, but he sounded very pleasant on the telephone.'

The merriness disappeared as if a veil had been whisked from Claire's eyes. And in its place came a hot eagerness for it to be him, followed by a cold mist of apprehension in case she let herself hope even for a second, and then had to face up to the prosaic truth that it was somebody else.

With shaking hands, she fixed the lid on the kettle and plugged it in. Then she turned, and said slowly, 'What gentleman, Mummy?'

It was Jake. It was! Her mother had written his name down on the little pad by the telephone: Mr Eagleton.

She hadn't even thought he had her number, but somehow he had got hold of it, and he had phoned her!

She was so crazy with excitement at the thought that it took her a moment to calm down enough to take in the rest of what her mother had to say. Jake had come near Winterton on business, he had told her mother, and he had wanted to call on Claire and make sure that she was fully recovered. Her mother had invited him to tea, but he had politely refused. Instead he was coming round at seven-thirty to take her out for a drink.

Less than three hours, and she would see him again! She could hardly believe it was true.

'It is all right, Claire, isn't it?' her mother asked anxiously. 'I know you wouldn't normally go out alone with anyone but Philip, but I thought, if this was someone who'd been with you on that terrible journey, it had to be right to make the arrangements for you. If you'd like Philip to come along too, I'm sure your father would agree to be on call for him this evening.'

'Oh, no,' Claire said, rather too vehemently.

'Well, it's up to you, dear.'

'It's fine, Mummy. Of course you did the right thing,'

'I was trying to remember whether you'd mentioned Mr Eagleton, Claire. I thought I might look out those videotapes Aunt Alice made of all the news items. Was he on those? I don't expect you'd remember, dear.'

He was. Claire had been shown them all by an insistent, beaming Aunt Alice as soon as she returned home, and she remembered the pictures all too well. There on the screen had been Jake, strong and dark and ruggedly handsome, his arm wrapped round her and his face bent to hers, hurrying her past the reporters as they left the airport. There had been Jake, fending off questions in the hotel lobby. Worst of all, there had been

Jake holding her hand as she stumbled her way through an interview with the BBC correspondent.

Her parents had seen them all too, of course, and at the time they didn't seem to have noticed the man who was so constantly at her side. But she didn't dare to risk rerunning the tape now, in case her mother might see those clasped hands, that strong arm around her, and lapse into a new load of loudly expressed doubts.

'He sat next to me on the plane,' she said shortly. 'But I haven't told you *my* news yet, Mummy. Would you believe it? The editor wants a new article from me!'

Why was Jake coming, why? What did he want with her, what would he say? Claire didn't even have a chance to ask herself these questions until after supper, and when she did have the chance she couldn't think of any coherent answers. Did he really feel the same way as she did? Had he been aching to see her again, aching so much that he'd finally decided to track her down and come and tell her how he felt? Or was there a more prosaic reason for his phone call? Was he just calling to make sure she was all right, as he had told her mother?

She was certainly aching to see him. Her heart seemed to be leaping and hammering inside her. She felt alive again, aware of herself and her body as she hadn't been at all since her return to Winterton.

That wasn't fair to Philip. She knew that, even though the knowledge didn't do anything to damp her excitement at the thought of seeing Jake. If only she had already broken off her relationship with Philip, she mourned, then she would have been free to explore any offer that Jake held out to her. As it was, she was still another man's girlfriend, and there would be absolutely no excuse for her and Jake behaving as they had done immediately after the hijack. Maybe that wasn't what he was thinking of anyway, she reminded herself.

How should she dress? She wanted to dress up to please Jake, to look beautiful and sexy, but she felt she couldn't wear anything too provocative in the circumstances. She wasn't going to wear the sort of clothes he had criticised before, though, so she picked out a pretty pink shirt-waister that really did fit her well. She unfastened her hair and brushed it vigorously, shaking it loose across her shoulders. That made her feel like Jake's girl, even if she didn't look all that different from the way Philip's girl normally looked.

A minute later she was back downstairs, chattering away to her parents with what felt like suspicious edginess as she waited anxiously for the doorbell to ring. It wasn't an easy conversation, because her mother and father had both been far more concerned than delighted at the news that she planned to persist with her career as a photo-journalist. It hadn't sunk into Claire's mind before that they had taken it for granted that she would abandon it after the hijacking, but now they made it very clear that it upset them to discover that this wasn't the case.

At last there was a buzz in the hallway. 'I'll go,' she said quickly, jumping to her feet.

She stopped in the hallway, took a deep breath, and opened the door.

Jake was standing there. Claire's breath seemed to leave her. She just stood for a long moment, feasting her eyes on him.

He was dressed in the dark suit he had worn on the plane, or one almost identical, and a smart grey shirt and tie. The piratical stubble was gone now, his deep tan had faded slightly, and his unruly dark hair was cut tamely short. She noticed all this, absorbed as she was in everything about him, but almost immediately her eyes were claimed and held by his clear grey gaze.

He held her look for a long time, without speaking. Suddenly it seemed irrelevant to ask why he had come, or what he wanted. All that mattered was that Jake was there, with her; that the two of them were together again.

'Claire?' her mother called questioningly from the living-room.

Claire came to her senses. 'You'd better come in,' she said in a low, unsteady voice.

'Thank you.'

She stepped aside, and Jake crossed the threshold. How strange, Claire thought, she had thought him totally alien when she met him at the resort, entirely different from all the men in Winterton, but now he seemed perfectly in place in her home.

He wasn't relaxed, though; she sensed that instinctively. She could remember the lazy confidence that had been her first impression of him, but now there was no trace of it. He was taut now, as if every move, every look, every word was held under tight control. That was understandable; the same tension seemed to grab at every muscle in Claire's body as she led him along the hallway and into the living-room where her parents were sitting.

Somehow she stumbled through the introductions. And then, to her relief, she had a chance to stay silent for a few minutes as her parents politely chatted to Jake, and he just as politely chatted back to them, explaining about the job that had brought him to Winterton: a survey for the site of a new factory, a few miles outside the town.

'You're quite recovered from the hijack now, then, Mr Eagleton?'

'Jake, please,' he dutifully corrected. 'Yes, thank you. I haven't forgotten any of it, of course, and it takes an effort of will to get on a plane nowadays. I'm sure you'll find that too, Claire. But otherwise, things are getting back to normal.' He turned to Claire, and his look surveyed her, though he didn't hold her eyes this time.

'You're looking well, Claire.'

'Thank you,' she whispered.

'Oh, Claire's fine, aren't you, dear?' her mother said cheerfully. 'Everything's been going swimmingly since she came back. We were so relieved to see her safe and sound, Philip especially. She'll have told you, I expect, about her boyfriend Philip? He's my husband's junior partner. They had been planning to get engaged at Christmas, but now they've decided not to wait so long, and they'll be making the announcement on Claire's birthday next month.'

'Engaged,' Jake said.

There was something bleak about Jake's tone. Claire opened her mouth to protest at this, to reassure him that it wasn't true. But it came to her, even before she spoke, that there really wasn't anything she could say. She couldn't contradict her mother outright without causing an awkward scene, and without making her feelings for Jake as well as for Philip all too apparent.

Nor was what her mother had said entirely an untruth. Both her parents really did believe that the engagement was going to go ahead, and now was hardly the time to explain to them about her continuing doubts.

She was still fumbling for a reply when Jake turned back to her and dutifully congratulated her on the engagement.

'We're not engaged yet.'

'But you are as good as engaged, aren't you, Claire? We're all so thrilled, Mr Eagleton. Not that we'd ever push Claire in any direction she wasn't happy to go, but I can tell you, it's been in my mind ever since Philip first came to work with Reggie.'

'That's understandable,' Jake said.

'And how about you, Mr Eagleton? You'll have a wife and children, I expect?'

'No.' Jake gave an awkward laugh. 'No, I guess I'm not the marrying kind.'

'Well, takes all sorts to fill a world, that's what I always say. So long as you're happy with your lot in life.'

'Don't mind Phyllis, Jake. She always talks nineteen to the dozen,' Claire's father said. 'Now, can I get you a drink before you and Claire set off? A whisky, perhaps, or a sherry?'

'That's very kind of you, but I'm driving, so I think I'd better not.' Jake turned back to Claire. 'Perhaps we should get going?'

'I'll just get my jacket.'

Claire went into the hall and reached for her linen jacket. She fumbled putting it on, her arms just wouldn't find the armholes. The scene with her parents had been so uncomfortable that it would be a relief to get away, but at the same time she was nervous about being alone with Jake. Engaged to Philip! That wasn't the impression she had wanted him to get, not at all. She wanted to explain to him that she had known ever since the hijack that she couldn't marry Philip, but she didn't know how to set about it when he had already been told the very reverse. She gave herself a last little shake, picked up her bag, and went back to the others.

'Well, it's been nice to meet you, Mrs Middleditch. And you, sir.' Jake shook hands with her parents.

'A pleasure. Do drop in again if you're in this part of the world.'

'Thank you.'

At last they were free. Claire pulled the front door to behind her, and paused on the step.

'Where to?' Jake asked.

Claire paused. She hadn't thought until then about this basic question.

'There's a pub not far away, the Gamekeeper. We could go there.'

'I've my car, so we don't need to go anywhere especially near.'

She glanced towards the road. That was Jake's, presumably, the silver BMW parked just outside the house. She could do as he suggested, drive somewhere with him. Sitting next to him in his car would be almost like being back on the plane again. She might turn to him in just the same way; he might smile at her, as she smiled at him; he might put his arms around her once more.

But where could they drive? And what would her and Philip's friends think, if any of them came across her and Jake in a quiet country pub miles from Winterton? It was tempting to take him somewhere where they could be private together, but it wouldn't be right. She shook her head. 'The Gamekeeper's quite nice. It's not far, we can walk.'

She set off down the road, and Jake fell in at her side. They didn't talk as they walked the few blocks to the Gamekeeper.

The lounge bar of the Gamekeeper was a pretty room, chintz-curtained and low-beamed. There were only a scattering of customers sitting at the oak tables, since it was still early evening. Claire and Jake found an empty table without difficulty.

'Lemonade?' Jake asked.

'Yes, please.'

He went to the bar, and Claire sat down. She watched his sturdy, powerful figure for a moment, walking away from her, then glanced around the room. She could see three or four friends and acquaintances, and she nodded and smiled at them. Her friend Lucy smiled back, then glanced at Jake and made a face as if to ask who he was. Claire pretended not to understand; she had no idea how to explain who Jake was and what he meant to her, and she certainly couldn't face another round of questions about the hijack.

Jake brought two glasses over to the table, set the lemonade down in front of her and the beer opposite, and sat down facing her. Claire looked at him. He didn't avoid her look, but his returning look seemed blank, shuttered even, as if he was intent on giving nothing of himself away to her. His grey eyes were opaque; even when they met hers full on, they seemed to convey no message.

This didn't seem like the man she had made love to with such abandon, Claire thought uneasily. This was the terse stranger who had said goodbye to her afterwards.

'So where's your boyfriend tonight?' he asked, in a harsh voice.

'He's on call, waiting in case there are any emergencies.'

'Does that mean he has to stay in?'

'He generally does.'

She expected Jake to pursue the line of conversation and ask her more about Philip, but instead he abruptly changed the subject.

'Are you giving up your work?'

'My journalism? No, of course not! In fact, I had some really good news, the chance of a new assignment, just today.'

'Did you? Tell me about it.'

Claire hesitated; she was still uneasy with him. Then the tension seemed to flow out of her. It would be so good to tell Jake her news. He wouldn't be as offhand about it as her parents had been, she thought. He would be genuinely glad for her, glad that she had been given a second chance. She leaned forward, setting her elbows on the table between them, and began to tell him about the meeting with John Wilkins.

Jake listened intently. He congratulated her, convincingly though not effusively, and then turned the conversation to a discussion of the sort of articles she might suggest writing.

They talked about this for a long time. Claire mentioned some of the ideas she had thought up that afternoon, and Jake commented on them, approving some and pointing out shortcomings in others. He also came up with several interesting ideas of his own, including a couple that Claire thought she might be able to use.

What a delight it was, Claire thought, to talk to somebody who didn't seem to think her choice of work weird, who understood why it attracted her. Jake didn't go on and on about things she couldn't do, he focused on things that she could, and he seemed to have a solid, realistic idea of her capabilities. She and Jake seemed to understand each other so easily, too. Even when she wasn't sure what she meant herself, he would pick up her thoughts and clarify them for her.

She had almost forgotten her earlier apprehension, completely forgotten that she had still to tell him about the real situation with Philip, when he said, 'So you'll be travelling abroad quite a bit, you reckon?'

'If everything works out this time, I hope I will. I've seen so little of the world, and I'd really like to do more travelling, go to strange places and meet different kinds of people.'

'And what does your Philip make of that?'

Claire went cold. She felt caught on the wrong foot, though she knew she should have guessed that Jake would harden the conversation at some point. He was a direct man; he had never shied off from awkward topics, and he had made it clear to her long before that he felt her combination of marriage and career plans was unrealistic.

'To be honest, he doesn't...'

'Claire! We haven't seen you for ages!'

The words, from behind Claire's back, were accompanied by footsteps and the bang of the door. Claire glanced around and saw her friend Alison standing there, with her boyfriend Mark just behind her.

'Hello, Alison,' she said awkwardly.

'Do you mind if we join you? We're not interrupting anything, are we?' Mark asked more calmly.

Claire hesitated. Mark and Alison *were* interrupting something, the first conversation she had had with Jake for a whole month. But she couldn't politely say that, and in any case she didn't want to rouse their curiosity about her relationship with Jake.

Too late. Alison was already reaching her hand across the table and introducing herself to Jake, who was standing to take it. A moment later both the newcomers were sitting at the table, and Jake had gone to the bar to get them drinks.

'What a gorgeous man,' Alison said, as soon as Jake was out of earshot. 'Where on earth did you meet him?'

Claire briefly explained who Jake was, and what he was doing in Winterton.

'Oh. So you haven't broken up with Philip, or...'

I wish I had, Claire thought. But she could hardly tell Alison about her doubts over Philip before she had made them clearer to Philip herself, so she said, 'Of course not,' and settled down to the usual sort of conversation about the goings-on of their mutual friends.

By the time Jake returned with the drinks, Alison was launched into a long tale about the local tennis club. Then more friends appeared, and Alison called them over, and before long the evening had turned into the sort of casual social gathering that Claire and Philip generally went to the pub to enjoy.

Jake seemed to get on well with all her friends, and they were careful to keep the conversation a step away from pure local gossip, so he certainly wasn't left out of it. In any other circumstances, Claire would have thought it a pleasant, enjoyable evening. But these were special circumstances; there were so many things she had wanted to say to Jake, and she simply couldn't say them in front of Alison and Mark and their friends. As the group settled in more and more comfortably, her mood drifted towards despair. She felt that everything that was being said was reinforcing Jake's impression that she and Philip were a firmly established couple, and that he was just a casual interloper.

It isn't like that at all! she wanted to tell him. I've already made one attempt to end my relationship with Philip, and, as soon as I have the opportunity to tell him without causing unnecessary hurt, I'm going to finish it for good. I know now that it wasn't just the hijack setting my emotions off balance; seeing you nearly a month afterwards, I feel just the same way about you as I did in the hotel. I don't love Philip, and never have. I know I'd be right to break with him, even if you decide that you don't want to take his place in my life.

But Alison chattered on, and none of this was said.

At last closing-time arrived. The group lingered, finishing their drinks, until the last minute, and then they all spilled out into the car park together.

'Coming back with us for coffee?' Alison asked.

'Not tonight.'

'Come round with Philip at the weekend, maybe?'

'I'll give you a call.'

'Yes, do. Nice to meet you, Jake.'

'And you,' Jake politely responded. He turned to Claire. 'It's this way back to your house?'

'That's right.'

They set off along the now darkened road. Claire waited until they were out of earshot of the others, then she said quietly, 'Jake, about Philip.'

'It's OK. You don't have to explain.'

She turned her head and looked at him, but in the darkness she couldn't make out his expression. 'But I want to explain,' she said lamely.

'Don't.'

The bluntness of this silenced her for a moment. Then she thought, and tried again.

'I didn't tell him about us.'

'That's your business,' Jake said brusquely. 'I don't want to know.'

All the same, Claire wanted to tell him. But she couldn't persist in the face of this opposition, and she couldn't help feeling that maybe Jake was telling the simple truth. He's never told you he loves you, she thought to herself. He didn't say that even when the two of you were making love. Maybe in a way he's relieved to discover—or at least, believe he's discovered—that what happened hasn't changed things with Philip. But, if he feels like that, why has he come? She couldn't understand it.

They walked the rest of the way in silence. They didn't stop at all until they came to where Jake's car was still parked in the road outside the house.

'Are you coming in again?' Claire asked.

'I'd rather not. Your parents won't think it rude? It's quite a way back to my hotel, so I'd rather get moving straight away.'

But I don't understand! Claire wanted to wail. We haven't said anything that matters to each other yet! If we leave it like this, I might never see you again! I want to tell you how I feel, I want to...

'You're sure you're OK?' Jake said in a low voice.

OK? How can I be OK, Claire thought, when I love you and you don't love me?

'It's been a month almost, I thought you'd be likely to know by now. But if you're not certain yet, I can give you my phone number. You must let me know if——'

If what? It came to Claire suddenly what he meant. If you're pregnant, he meant. So that was why he had come—because he too had realised how rash they had been, and he too had been worried in case there were consequences to be faced up to.

And she had thought he wanted to see her—to see her, Claire, because he might care for her and miss her just as she cared for and missed him! It wasn't that at all. She could see it now. He had just been doing his duty, making sure that everything was all right, tidying up an inconvenient loose end.

'No,' she said in a voice that came out as stiff as a frozen sheet. 'It's quite all right. There's nothing to worry about.'

'I'm glad. I hadn't wanted it to change anything between you and Philip.'

He paused, as if he was expecting her to assure him that it hadn't. But how could she? Even if he didn't care about her at all, she couldn't help feeling as she did about him. It had changed everything, even if he would never know it.

And he wouldn't, because she had more pride than to say anything to him now. She stood there awkwardly, looking downwards, until a series of little rustlings told her that Jake had found his car keys. He unlocked the car door, then turned back to her.

'Goodbye, Claire.'

His voice seemed unexpectedly gentle; there was none of the harshness that had been in it earlier. Claire looked up, suddenly disarmed, and met his eyes.

Jake reached forward. He caught at her wrists and gently pulled her towards him, with hands apart. He bent forwards and swiftly, lightly, deposited a kiss on her mouth.

For a moment they stood there, staring at each other in the dim light. Then Jake's mouth came down again, hard, on Claire's, and the world seemed to revolve around her.

The kiss was fierce, but it was brief; in a few seconds he was releasing her and she was staggering backwards, knocked off balance in every sense by his embrace. All her careful rationalisations seemed to have been shattered. He does want me, he does! she thought with sudden, intense clarity. He wants me just as badly as I want him.

But, before she could collect herself and say any of this, Jake had climbed into the car and was revving it up. 'Goodbye,' he said again, though it was little more than a mutter over the sound of the car engine. Claire had not had time even to start a reply, to protest, to plead, before he wrenched the car into gear and was roaring away into the night.

CHAPTER TEN

THE following day dragged at the boutique. Claire did wonder if she should hand in her notice. She decided to tell Mrs James about the editor's offer as soon as she came in. But Mrs James wouldn't ask for her resignation, she suspected. She had always been an easygoing employer, happy to allow Claire unpaid time off in their quiet season. Though Claire didn't want to work in the boutique forever, she knew she hadn't yet successfully completed even one major assignment as a photojournalist, and that it made sense to keep the boutique job as a kind of safety net until it was clearer how things were going to work out.

At least things were clearer in her own mind now. She was convinced that it would be a mistake to get engaged to Philip, and there obviously wasn't any prospect of her seeing more of Jake. So she would concentrate on her career.

Perhaps Jake had been right, she thought. Perhaps she would never manage to combine career and marriage successfully. Perhaps she would never have to try. If she turned down Philip, she might never marry at all. Did she mind that thought? She honestly didn't know. Her heart was so full of the misery of Jake's rejection, the thought of ever marrying anyone else seemed incredible to her.

Philip rang from his surgery towards the end of the morning, and Claire confirmed their arrangement to go out for a drink that evening. She would tell him about her possible new assignment then, she thought, and somehow she would tell him too that she could never marry him. Then, very soon, she would try to make arrangements to move away from Winterton. That was only fair, she felt, since Philip's job would keep him in the town. Anyway, the kind of work she would be looking for wasn't to be found in Winterton. The place to live, if she really meant to focus on her career, was definitely London.

'Let me get this straight,' Philip said coldly. 'You went to London, to the newspaper offices, to explain how you came to lose your photographs and mess up your great assignment as a photo-journalist.'

Claire stared at him. And she had been wondering how she might work up an argument over the assignment! It would have been much harder to avoid one, she realised, amazed—Philip was already spoiling for a fight over it.

'*Lose* my photographs?' she repeated. '*Mess up* my assignment? I worked damn hard at that assignment, Philip! If it hadn't been for the hijack—and you can't tell me that was my fault!—it would have gone perfectly well. I didn't carelessly lose my photos, they were destroyed! And it wasn't me who messed things up, it was the hijackers! John Wilkins understood that, even if you can't!'

'That's not my point,' Philip retorted majestically. 'You went to that office to provide an explanation and an apology, and you left planning to do some more work for the paper.'

'That's right. John Wilkins offered me another chance because he understood that the problems with that assignment hadn't been my fault at all.'

'And you took it!'

'Of course I did!' Claire responded.

'Well, you shouldn't have!'

This remark fell into a dead silence. After a moment, Philip seemed to realise that the silence didn't have precisely the quality he was aiming for, and he added, 'Not without consulting me first, that is.'

'Consulting you? But, Philip, you don't know anything about photo-journalism!'

'But I do know about you, Claire. I know about us. And I know that after the terrible mess you got yourself into last time, I'm never going to allow you to work abroad again.'

'Never going to allow me?' Claire repeated, genuinely amazed.

'Never.' Philip was getting into his stride now. 'I always knew it was a mistake letting you go on that assignment,' he went on inexorably. 'A girl like you, travelling abroad on her own! Totally unsuitable. If you really want to travel, Claire, I'm sure we'll be able to arrange something. They do some excellent package holidays these days. Once I'm well-established, I should be able to take two or even three weeks' holiday at a time. I'll take you wherever you want to go. But as for this photo-journalism, I forbid you to carry on with it.'

'You forbid me?' Claire screamed back, oblivious by now of the curious glances of the other customers of the Gamekeeper. 'You've no right to forbid me to do anything, Philip Anderson!'

'I have every right, since you are going to marry me.'

Claire opened her mouth to scream again, then thought, and closed it. A moment later she said, more rationally, 'So that's what marriage means to you: forbidding me to do things you don't approve of.'

'Marriage means looking after you,' Philip said sturdily. 'I shall do anything and everything I think necessary to that end. And if you make plans to do something that's stupid or dangerous, then of course I shall forbid it.'

'That isn't what marriage means to me, Philip. I always thought marriage ought to be a partnership. You discuss plans and ideas with your partner, but one partner doesn't *forbid* the other to do anything.'

Now it was Philip's turn to think.

'A partnership, yes,' he agreed. 'But you have to understand, Claire, that I shall always be the senior partner.'

Claire silently shook her head.

'That isn't what I want, Philip.'

'I don't understand you, Claire. Any man in my position would say the same. No sane man would stand for his wife, his fiancée or even his girlfriend jetting off alone around the world. OK, I tolerated your accepting your prize commission, but that was to give you a chance to see for yourself that it wasn't the life for you. And heavens, the hijacking brought that home much more forcefully than I had ever expected! But now you have to accept the lesson you learned. It's time to put this pipe-dream behind you, and settle down to making wedding plans.'

Any man? Claire asked herself. *Would* any man forbid her to do as she wanted? Did *all* husbands boss their wives around in this blatant way? Perhaps Philip was right; perhaps they did.

You've learned your lesson, Philip had said, and she had. But the lesson she had learned wasn't that she must submit to a man. She had learned instead that if marriage was only available on those terms, she didn't want it. She would have welcomed a loving partner—provided it was the right partner for her—but she certainly wasn't ready to abdicate responsibility for her own actions and choices.

'I'm not sure that I want to marry, Philip.'

'Don't be ridiculous, Claire,' Philip said brusquely. 'You're acting like a spoilt child who's been told she can't have a second ice-cream. Grow up, for heaven's sake!'

But I am, Claire thought silently. You don't realise how fast I am growing up.

'I think it would be a mistake for us to marry. Maybe I shouldn't marry anyone, I don't know. But I do know that I can't marry you, Philip.' Claire hesitated for a moment, then added lamely, 'I'm sorry.'

Philip stared at her. At last he said, 'You want some more time to think.'

'No. I've already thought hard about this, Philip, and I've made my decision now.'

'Perhaps I have been hurrying you. Entirely understandable, I think, in the circumstances, but I can see now that it might not have been for the best. We should have kept to our original timetable. An engagement at Christmas, and a wedding next year. Of course, if that's what you want, I'll go along with it. I'm disappointed, naturally, but I think it's true to say that I understand. You'll never find me less than sympathetic to you, Claire.'

I'll never find you listening to me! Claire thought, in a moment of sheer despair. But she couldn't afford to be ambiguous this time. She didn't want to leave Philip any illusions, or to be dragged back into a relationship with him through sheer inertia.

'I thought I'd look for a flat in London,' she said. 'I've some money my grandfather left me, that would help me to get started, to keep going until I can be sure of paying my own way. The work's all in London, of course. All the papers and magazines are there. It really doesn't make any sense for me to stay in Winterton.'

'A flat in London!'

Claire had never seen Philip so amazed, or so much at a loss. He shook his head in sheer bewilderment.

'I'll never understand you, Claire.'

How true, thought Claire. You won't.

Claire told her parents her decision that same evening, after Philip had returned her to her doorstep. She was expecting them to be surprised, disappointed—angry, even.

They were surprised, that was obvious. They had taken it for granted for so long that Claire and Philip would marry that they hadn't seen any of the earlier signs of Claire's change of heart. Her mother at least was disappointed, too; she had been looking forward to having grandchildren very soon.

But they weren't angry. That surprised Claire almost as much as it relieved her. Her parents didn't boss her, she thought to herself; they didn't go in for insisting and forbidding. Their marriage seemed to her to be much more of a true partnership than the arrangement Philip had outlined to her.

And in a way both her father and her mother were relieved that she had solved the dilemma of combining marriage and career. It wouldn't have worked, they assured her, to try to pursue her career as a photo-journalist while she was planning to marry Philip. It would take single-minded dedication if she were to try to reach the top. They were surprised that she had made the decision to try, and they suggested—very gently—that when the right man came along she might find herself reviewing that decision. But in the meantime they promised her their full support.

And in the weeks that followed they gave it. They discussed her plans for new articles with her, and made suggestions just as thoughtful, and almost as incisive, as Jake's had been. They went over her finances, and made sure that she would be able not only to pay her rent, but to eat properly too. Her mother helped her to go round looking at suitable apartments in London, and together they found the ideal base for her to live and work from.

It was a tiny studio flat, up umpteen flights of steps, but its single room was good-sized and very well-lit. Claire could see immediately how she would do it out, and within a few weeks she had it just as she wanted it. The walls were painted white, to make the flat seem even lighter. She covered them with blown-up photographs— some of her own, and some by other photographers whose work she admired—in simple black frames. She bought a second-hand divan, and smothered it in cushions so that it would double as a sofa in daytime. A big working-table set under the dormer window, two beech chairs with satisfyingly curved arms, and a couple of gaily striped kelims on the polished wood floor completed the furnishings.

But the glory of the flat was its view. It was only of London rooftops, plain clay tiles most of them, but somehow this particular selection had a satisfying pattern. The narrow streets intersected not in a grid, but in a complex pattern of angles broad and acute, and the varying height of the buildings added yet another dimension of complexity.

It was a view that cried out to be photographed, and Claire did her best to do justice to it. She photographed it in sunlight; on wet days, with rain glistening on the tiles; underlit by a weak sun beneath stormclouds; in the early evening with the streetlights shining; when winter came, with a deep fall of snow hiding the tiles and cresting the chimney-pots.

This work—indeed, all her work—was a source of great satisfaction to her. John Wilkins accepted one of her suggestions for an article, and it was published almost unchanged. He accepted some other, later suggestions too, though others still he turned down. Claire felt a special loyalty to the *Sunday Tribune*, since John Wilkins had given her her first big break, but soon her work began to be seen by other editors, and she had as many offers of work as she could handle. Not all of it was prestigious or well-paid, and some of it was from publications that clearly ran on a shoestring, but by working hard she found she could just about pay her way without dipping into her savings. Though she knew it would take a long time before she reached the top of her profession, she felt she had made a satisfying start to her career.

Personally, too, her life began take on a new shape. Her growing success gave her confidence. It no longer seemed strange to take pride in herself or her appearance; all the people she met in her new life seemed to dress with a style and flair that was underpinned by physical awareness. She started to pick clothes in brighter colours and, though she rejected the idea of cutting her hair, she abandoned her ponytail for good.

At first she travelled every free weekend back to Winterton, to see her parents and her old friends. But then the invitations came snowing in from new friends in London, and it was an effort to keep even one weekend a month free to see her parents.

There were men among her new friends, many men, some of them highly eligible and most of them good fun to be with. She soon knew beyond a trace of doubt that she had been right not to marry Philip; the easy, flexible life-style of her new acquaintances suited her far better than Philip's rigid attitudes ever had done. But, though she enjoyed carefree evenings with her new friends, no one man ever erased the memory of Jake, or really touched her heart.

That was just as well, she told herself. She was a career girl. She knew that now. If her career didn't mesh with marriage, then that was no problem. She was confident now that she would never choose to marry.

Cautiously, with one elbow, Claire pushed down the handle of her bathroom door. She nudged the door open, and made her way out into the living-area.

The light streaming through the big window seemed alarmingly bright after the gloom of her improvised darkroom. She blinked a few times, then walked over to the table under the window. Carefully she deposited on it the photographs that she had been holding in her hands.

The contact sheet hadn't deceived her, she had got it right! There was the bay, exactly as she remembered it. The sky looked so blue, the sand of the beach so clean and white, the mountains so broodingly powerful, that she could practically imagine herself there again, standing on the hotel balcony with the hot sun beating down on her shoulders.

These could almost have been the photographs she had taken on Jake Eagleton's balcony, more than a year earlier, but they weren't. The great white bulk of the new hotel, looming up on the slope behind the harbour, was proof of the time that had passed since her first visit to the little resort. Otherwise, though, very little had changed.

She had changed, though—changed a lot. She wore a pink blouse that hugged her figure, showing off her slim waist, and the swirling width of her cerise-coloured skirt emphasised her shapely legs. A flamboyant slide, covered in enamelled flowers, pinned the long honey-coloured swirl of her hair back at one side. The way she stood, tall and straight, underlined her new self-confidence.

A year before, she thought with light amusement, she had been such a bungling amateur! Knocking on doors, indeed, without stopping to think of a better way to get her pictures! She had thought it the height of in-trepidity, and in retrospect it had been, but it certainly hadn't been a professional way to go about her work. This time she had shown her Press card to the hotel manager, and one of the chambermaids had obligingly let her into an empty room.

Her cuttings file was thick now; this would be very far from the first big article she had once intended it to be. All the same, it was special to her. She had steeled herself to fly again months earlier, but even so it had taken all the strength she possessed to go back on the same route, and replace the photographs that the airport police had destroyed. She had given herself a year before trying, and even then it hadn't been easy to face the memories, but she was a professional now, she had known she was strong enough to do it, and she had been!

John Wilkins would like the piece, she thought, not only because he knew it mattered to her, but because it would be good, very good. It wouldn't end up spiked, it would be published in the *Sunday Tribune* colour supplement. Maybe, who knew, Jake Eagleton would see it. He might look at the view that was almost, but not quite, the view he had seen from his hotel balcony the year before, and perhaps, for a moment at least, he would stop to think of the eager, awkward girl who had barged into his life, and then left it forever.

No good thinking about that. There was room for friends in her life, but there wasn't any room for a special man. And there hadn't been room for a special woman in Jake Eagleton's life either, had there? Many things had changed in a year, but that surely hadn't. It would have to be Claire's private grief that, though her outward self had changed so much, her inner feelings about Jake didn't seem to have changed at all.

Forget him, she told herself, there was work to be done, deadlines to be met. She sat down at the table, took out her magnifying glass, and began to think about which photographs she wanted to show John Wilkins, and how they might be cropped to illustrate her article.

'Claire?'

The voice at the end of the phone line was familiar; it was John Wilkins's secretary calling.

'Hello, Lorna,' Claire responded.

'It's nothing urgent, Claire, just a message to pass on. We had a phone call for you here at the *Tribune*, and since it's not company policy to pass out freelance journalists' addresses or phone numbers, I'm calling to let you know about it.'

'Fine,' Claire agreed. Though the policy sometimes proved inconvenient, she appreciated the security aspect of it, and was always happy to call back when people made enquiries about her work. 'Who rang? Anyone I'd have heard of?'

'It wasn't a work call, Claire—at least, I don't think it was. It was a man who said he used to know you. He'd seen the travel piece we printed last week, and he wanted a word with you, he said.'

A little prickle of apprehension tickled Claire's spine. 'Got a name and number, Lorna?'

'Yes, it's here. The name's Jake Eagleton, and here's the number.' She read it out to Claire. 'Ring a bell?'

'Sort of,' Claire said edgily.

'I can leave it to you to deal with, then?'

'Sure, Lorna.'

'That's fine. How's the baby-show piece coming along?'

For the next few minutes they chatted, as casually as Claire could manage, about the next article she was preparing for John Wilkins. Then at last Lorna said goodbye, and Claire could put down the phone and look at the number scrawled on her pad.

She hadn't written down Jake's name. No need, she would never forget that! But he had never given her his phone number, so that was unfamiliar to her. Where was his house? she wondered. Or was it a flat? He had never told her that, either.

And, more to the point, why on earth had he telephoned her after seeing the article in the *Tribune*? She might have idly thought that he might see it and think of her, but she had never, never imagined that he would use it as a reason to get back in contact with her.

Was she glad? She wasn't sure. After a year of carefully rebuilding her life after the emotional devastation wrought by the hijack, it was an unnerving thought that Jake Eagleton might be about to come back into it. As attractive as ever, doubtless—and as footloose as ever, too.

She could have thought it over for weeks, and still been no closer to deciding what she felt about it. But she couldn't afford to spend weeks thinking about Jake, so she resolved her dilemma brutally, by picking up the telephone again. She dialled the number briskly, without giving herself any space for second thoughts.

She could hear his phone ringing, echoing down the line. She counted twenty rings before she came to the conclusion that Jake wasn't going to answer. Curse him! She had got all psyched up to talk to him, and now she wasn't going to be able to. She put the phone down and tried to get on with the article she was writing, but somehow the words just wouldn't flow on to the paper as she'd intended.

That evening she had a date, and she wasn't prepared to phone Jake immediately before leaving, and risk being upset only moments before seeing other people. So it was the following morning before she eventually dialled his number again—and he answered.

'Eagleton,' he said in a brusque, professional voice.

'Jake? Jake, it's Claire.'

Their conversation stumbled on through a rocky stretch of platitudes. He explained how hard he had found it to get hold of her, and he politely praised the article and her photographs. No, Claire agreed, the resort hadn't changed much. Yes, it had been difficult going back, at least in patches: she had felt apprehensive buying the travel tickets, and positively scared getting on the plane at the airport, but she was glad to have finally finished the old assignment.

Jake said tersely, 'So you're a full-time photo-journalist now.'

Oh, yes. I quit my job in the boutique not long after I las. saw you. I've done quite a few pieces for the *Tribune*, and I work for a couple of magazines...' She mentioned some of the names to him.

'I rarely see any of them,' Jake said. 'I only picked up the *Tribune* by chance at a friend's house, or I wouldn't have seen your travel piece.'

'I'm glad you did.'

'Yes. So you use your maiden name still for writing under?'

Even though she was nervous herself, Claire could sense the tight edge in Jake's voice. 'Jake,' she said gently, 'that's the only name I have.'

'So you didn't marry your doctor?'

'No. No, I didn't marry Philip.'

'Because of your work?'

'Partly,' she said carefully. 'I suppose you were right, it isn't a job that would mesh well with marriage.'

'You live alone, then?'

'Yes, in North London.' She named the nearby main road to him.

'Then we're—oh, two, three miles apart. No more than that.'

'I hadn't realised.'

'Nor had I.'

There was an awkward silence, then Jake went on, 'Could we meet up some time? Just to talk things over? One evening, perhaps. There's a little bistro round the corner where I often go; maybe we could eat there.'

'That would be nice,' Claire said.

'Could you manage this Friday?'

'This Friday. I'm not sure, let me see...'

Her diary was in her handbag, and she reached for it and rummaged through the pages. It was full, very full; though Claire quite enjoyed living alone, she didn't like spending evenings alone in the slightest, and when she wasn't planning working-trips she often found herself solidly booked up two or three weeks ahead.

'Not Friday, I'm afraid,' she said. 'I could manage next Tuesday...'

'No good. I'll be in Rome then.'

It took them several minutes—and a private decision by Claire to cancel a dinner-date that a persistent admirer had talked her into—before they managed to settle on a date ten days from then. A few more platitudes, and they parted with mutual assurances that they would look forward to it.

Claire did look forward to it, now it was fixed. It might not be wise to let Jake into her life again, she thought, but all the same it had given her a warm feeling to hear his rich-toned northern drawl. It would be even nicer to see him.

But it would be nothing more than a dinner, she told herself firmly. How could it be? What she had told him was true: her life-style now really wouldn't fit in well with a permanent commitment to another person. And nor would his. Jake had always been footloose, travelling alone. The only thing that had changed between them was that now Claire was in the same situation.

CHAPTER ELEVEN

Two minutes past eight. Claire could hear heavy male footsteps ascending the flights of stairs that led to her front door. Nearer, and nearer.

She sat on her chair by the window, without thinking of going to open the door. The doorbell rang. She counted to ten, then stood up and went to answer it.

There was Jake. She stood there for a moment, looking at him. He was wearing a casual suede jacket, dark brown jumper and matching trousers, and holding a large bunch of white roses in his hand. He looked so—so like Jake, that she couldn't help a shiver of delighted anticipation passing through her.

'Hello, Claire,' Jake said in a low, slightly husky voice, holding out the roses.

'They're for me?' she said stupidly.

'Definitely for you.' And there was the smile she remembered, that lazy, wide one that spread across his face and brought a warmth to the cool grey of his eyes. She could feel its impact like a touch, spreading warmly across her skin.

'Thank you. I'll... Do come in,' she finished in a rush.

'Thanks, I will.'

'I'll just put these in some water.'

She hunted under the sink for a vase. All the time she was acutely conscious of Jake's presence. He seemed to be looking around the room, but every so often she was conscious of his breaking the rhythm of his methodical examination, and of his eyes moving to her. He wasn't staring, wasn't letting his look linger, but she knew that he was just as aware of her as she was of him.

The room wasn't all that large, and it didn't take Jake long to take in all the details. His eyes rested finally on the table beneath the window, cluttered with all the tools of Claire's work in progress.

As she was hastily fitting the white roses into a chunky green pottery vase, she sensed him striding across to the table. She turned to see what had caught his eye. He wasn't looking at her work. He was gazing beyond the table, at the view out of her window.

She crossed the room to join him.

'It's hardly a classic view,' she said awkwardly. 'Not sea or mountains or...'

'Nonsense. Rooftops are as pleasing in their way as anything else. Have you taken any photos of it?'

'Yes, I have, actually.' Claire reached past him to the map cabinet that she used for storing her prints, and pulled open a drawer. 'These haven't been published, but I've taken quite a lot.'

She pulled out a sheaf and worked quickly through it, picking out half a dozen of the most successful prints and spreading them right across her work-table, over the pile of typescripts and negatives and unanswered letters. She reached down to switch on an angled light so that Jake would be able to see them clearly.

He looked for several minutes in silence, picking up one or two of the prints and holding them closer to the light so that he could see the details. Finally he turned and looked at Claire.

'These are good,' he said. 'Very good.'

'Thank you.'

'Have you ever thought of exhibiting? There must be a few galleries around that specialise in this kind of photography.'

'I haven't yet, but it's something I'd like to consider doing one day. When I'm a bit more established, and some of the pressure eases.'

'You should.'

There was a moment's silence. Claire looked at Jake; Jake looked at Claire. This wasn't the shuttered stranger who had said goodbye so awkwardly to her a year earlier, this was the man who had made love to her immediately after the hijack. The thought flowered in Claire's mind, and with it a memory of his touch, of the glory of their lovemaking, and a sudden desperate urge to be naked in his arms once more.

It was too soon; he was still too much of a stranger to her. And he seemed to sense that too, for an instant later he had torn away his gaze, and was saying, in a brusque voice, 'I booked for eight-thirty, so we should get going.'

His car was waiting outside—a BMW very similar to the one he had driven the year before, but a new model. He saw her into the passenger seat and took the wheel himself.

Claire shot a few cautious glances at him while he was driving. Now she could see that her memory of him hadn't been as totally reliable as she had first thought. Her most enduring impression had been one of ruggedness, of the sheer dependable strength of Jake during the ordeal of the hijack. But that had been an impression partly forged by the circumstances; the strain of that experience had affected him just as it had affected her. That strain had eased now, and she could see in him much more of the easy, relaxed manner that he had shown when they had first met.

He had a good sense of humour too, she thought, reminiscing. She liked that in him, and she liked his open interest in her—in people generally, she suspected. But the greatest shock was in being reminded of the sheer maleness of him. There was an almost animal sensuality about his movements, his expression, that seemed just as powerful when she set him against her present boyfriends as it had been a year before, when she had had only Philip to compare him with.

She had been close to thinking it irrational that Jake Eagleton should stick so stubbornly in her mind, but it didn't seem at all irrational to her then. It was a devastatingly accurate reflection of the impact he still had on her.

'We'll have to park around the corner,' said Jake, swinging the BMW into a side street, 'and walk back.'

He parked—not impatiently, but with the careful attention he seemed to show to everything he did—and walked round to open her door. He took her hand as he helped her out of the car, and kept on holding it as they walked the few yards to the little bistro.

A few minutes later they were comfortably seated at a corner table, with drinks in front of them, gazing at each other over the clutter of flowers and candlesticks.

In some ways, the year that had intervened since their last meeting seemed to have melted away. They had the same easy understanding of each other that they had had all along. And in his laid back way Jake had considerable charm: whenever things threatened to become prickly he eased them back into a smooth path.

But they did threaten to become prickly. Indeed, they were prickly already. Claire couldn't help being conscious of her intense physical attraction to Jake, and of the occasional unguarded look and gesture that showed her it was still fully returned. And she couldn't decide what she wanted to do about it.

It was easy to say that she wanted him as a lover. In a purely physical sense, that was true. But she had never been a girl who went in for casual love-affairs. The many men who had enjoyed her company over the previous year had none of them passed her bedroom door, and the thought of a casual affair appealed just then no more than it ever had. Anyway, her feelings for Jake weren't casual, and she felt, instinctively, that she would never be able to confine him to a neat corner of her life.

If he was to play any part at all in her life, she wanted him to be at the very centre of it. But she already had a centre to her life in her career, and Jake already had one in his career. So what could he offer to her, what could she offer to him, that they might find it possible to accept? She simply didn't know.

Nor did Jake show any inclination to raise this tricky subject. Instead, he made every effort to keep the conversation light and friendly. They talked about Claire's work, the assignments she planned and the people she was working with; they talked about Jake's work, which was also going well. He told some entertaining stories about incidents on his travels, and prised some anecdotes out of Claire too.

If it had been anyone but Jake, Claire would have reckoned the evening a great success. But this wasn't anyone else, this was Jake, the man she had loved and maybe still loved, and she felt that there was something false about treating him as a charming stranger. It felt to her as if his façade would have to fall before the evening was over; but the evening drew on, and there was no repetition of the moment by the window in her apartment, when she had sensed his guard dropping.

At the end of the evening, he refused her offer of a coffee back at her flat and dropped her at the door without more than the lightest touch of a goodnight kiss—and without making any suggestion that they might meet again.

In a way, Claire wasn't surprised. But oh, it hurt. When she got up the stairs to her flat she slammed the front door behind her, and threw herself face-forward on to the pile of cushions that littered her divan.

He just thinks the same as you do, she told herself sharply: that in spite of your attraction to each other it could never work. He was wrong to contact you again, he's right to break things off here. But, though she told herself this, and told herself repeatedly that there was no room for Jake Eagleton in her full, happy, successful life, she couldn't help being conscious of a void at the centre of her life that she never normally noticed.

Was this really what she wanted? she asked herself, unhappily. To be a single career woman forever, to abandon any thought of marriage and children for the sake of a camera and an endless series of plane tickets? Her career was undeniably rewarding, but just then she felt that, if she had to make that kind of sacrifice in order to develop it, it could never be worth it.

But there wasn't any alternative, she reminded herself. Jake hadn't made any kind of offer to her, he hadn't even suggested a love-affair, and marriage was certainly right out of his book. It wasn't only her career that created a barrier between them, it was his career, too.

She forced herself to get up, made a strong cup of black coffee, and played a dozen records before she went to bed. All the time she couldn't help wishing that Jake was there to listen to them with her.

Two weeks later, Jake phoned again. He suggested that they see a film together, a new smash hit that had opened the week before.

Claire found herself leafing through her diary and accepting the invitation almost automatically. It was only once he had rung off that she admitted to herself that she was surprised to have heard from him, and that she wasn't at all sure she was doing the right thing in agreeing to see him again. Who was she agreeing to see? The lover she had lost, or the distant, hurtful stranger who hid that lover from her?

She saw the stranger. The two of them spent a pleasant but low-key evening together, without ever pursuing an intimate conversation or touching each other lovingly. There were several moments when Claire sensed that Jake was close to making an attempt to rekindle the passion between them, but every time he seemed to shy away. He barely touched her hand, and didn't kiss her even once.

He phoned again the following week, and took Claire to the theatre. Then he didn't call her for a month.

Claire wouldn't have found this unusual if he had been any of her other boyfriends. Many of them travelled extensively, and were sometimes away from town for weeks on end. But he wasn't another boyfriend, he was Jake.

And, though she knew she had acted the stranger to him just as much as he had done to her, inside she didn't feel like that at all. They had only had three dates, but already she was getting in the habit of waiting by the phone for him to call. Her other boyfriends seemed to have lost all their appeal, and she had turned down several dates that she would previously have accepted without a second thought. Even her work was suffering. She would sit at her work-table and dream of Jake when she was supposed to be preparing her copy; she wasn't being as assiduous as usual in chasing up the leads she was given and finding more work.

Would he call again? Did he plan to keep on calling her up every few weeks, and taking her out casually? She hated every moment when the phone didn't ring, even grew impatient when friends chatted for too long in case Jake was trying to phone her and couldn't get through, but at the same time she knew that she couldn't cope with that. Jake's effect on her wasn't comparable with the effect of the many easygoing swains she never thought of between one date and the next. She couldn't tone down her feelings to order. If she saw him at all, she knew that he was going to dominate her entire life. If they were to have any relationship at all, she wanted it to be an intense and passionate love-affair. But then, that was the very thing that their lives couldn't hold. Wasn't it?

At last Jake called, late one night. 'I've been abroad,' he said. 'And now I'm back for two, maybe three weeks. When can you see me?'

Claire didn't answer immediately. A part of her heart was crying out, 'Today!', but another part shouted, just as insistently, 'Never!'

'Jake,' she said very quietly, 'I'm not sure that I should see you again.'

'Not——'

There was a heavy silence. Then Jake said, in a sharp voice, 'There's someone else.'

'No, not at all. It's not that. It's just that...' Her voice tailed off, because she couldn't think how to explain her reservations to him.

'Look, we have to talk. Meet me once more, at least, and we'll talk about it.'

Hesitantly, Claire agreed to dinner in a couple of days' time.

Claire buried herself in work for those two days, obsessively revising and re-revising everything she wrote, and taking on at least three too many new assignments. She did everything she could to keep her mind off Jake, but every time she eased her pace she found herself thinking about him.

Was this *really* what he wanted, to see her casually, only when it suited him, as just one of many friends? She knew she didn't want that. But was there any other kind of relationship between them that Jake might suggest, and that she would wish to accept? Only marriage, she thought unhappily, and she couldn't believe that he would ever offer her that.

Finally the evening of their date came round. Jake took her to a different place this time, a small French restaurant with dim lighting and atmospheric music.

The setting seemed to Claire more romantic than any of the places where they had met since the hijack. It wasn't anything like the little restaurant by the harbour where they had first dined together, but in a strange way it reminded her of that night.

She had barely known Jake then, she thought to herself, and yet in some strange way she had sensed even then that this was what she wanted most of all: to look up, and see him sitting opposite her.

She looked. He was soberly dressed, in a dark suit and blue shirt that seemed to tame his pirate nature. His hair had grown a little, and a loose lock fell over his forehead. She ached to reach out and touch it. His expression held just a hint of a frown, and his capable hands were playing with an empty glass. He was tanned again, from his trip presumably, and but for the formal clothes he looked very much as he had looked when she had first met him.

Strength, that was the impression he gave, she thought to herself. Strength and confidence. He wasn't a conventionally 'safe' man, he had always given off an air of dangerous abandonment, but all the same she felt safe with him. He had his own nature under control, and he seemed to be firmly in control of everything else that happened to him. They could face the best and worst of things together, she thought. Whatever happened to her, she would rather have Jake at her side than anyone else she knew.

She had been trying to convince herself that this evening she would persuade him that it was over, that she didn't want to see him again. But now, she didn't think she would ever have the strength to do that.

'Let's eat first,' Jake said. 'We'll have plenty of time to talk afterwards.'

They ate—a delicious meal of grilled shrimps followed by peppered steak, though Claire was feeling too tense to enjoy it as much as she would have done at any other time. And they drank, though not too much. All the time, as they sat opposite each other and Jake talked, casually and amusingly, of things that didn't matter to either of them, Claire kept thinking to herself, I love him. I do want him in my life, even if it has to be on his terms, and whatever the cost. And then she thought, but the cost is too high, and I shall never be able to afford it.

The waiter cleared away their cheese, and the coffee came.

'Can I talk first?' Jake asked.

'If you like.'

'Yes, I would.' He took a deep breath, and ran a hand nervously through his unruly shock of hair. 'I didn't know what I had in mind when I tried to contact you again, Claire. I simply felt that I had to see you again, just once more. And then I told myself that there wasn't any room for you in my life, and not much more for me in yours, but all the same I knew I had to see you again, and then again. Every time I told myself I ought to leave you without making another date, and every time, after I left you, I could hardly wait to phone and arrange to see you again. Then, when you told me that you didn't want to see me any more, I realised how much you meant to me. I'd kept on telling myself that the answer was to keep it cool, to not get too involved. But I am involved. I can't do without you.'

Claire's hands were trembling. She put them in her lap and squeezed them together.

'I love you, Claire.'

'I love you, too,' she whispered.

'And it won't do to keep on seeing each other like this, will it?'

She silently shook her head.

'So we'll have to work out something else.'

A bubble of pleasure and relief seemed to rise inside Claire. But at the same time she didn't dare to let herself hope for something that wouldn't be possible. 'But, Jake,' she said gently, 'there isn't . . .'

'Yes, there is.' Jake said firmly. 'There aren't any easy answers, we both know that. But if we both want to badly enough, I think we might be able to work something out.'

'You mean...'

'I mean getting married,' Jake said in a rush. He shook his head, as if he could hardly believe what he had said. He brushed his hair back from his forehead again, with an awkward movement of his hand. 'I've always said I never would,' he went on abruptly. 'I've never thought seriously about it before. But I was so relieved when you told me you weren't married to your doctor. You'll want to get married, every woman does. And when I imagine you marrying someone else one day, the thought makes me sick. You can't do that. You've got to marry me.'

'Jake,' Claire said, with a nervous half-laugh, 'I haven't *got* to marry anyone.'

'Well, I want you to marry me. Claire, it wouldn't work unless we were married. I don't want to be just one of the men you see now and then, when you're around and I'm around in the same place. I want to be at the centre of your life. I want trust and commitment. I want marriage.'

'But you always reckoned that it couldn't work like that. That when men in your position got married, it led to unhappiness.'

'It can, I know.' Jake frowned, his heavy brows lowering over his darkening grey eyes. 'I won't say I like the thought of your job,' he said. 'I guess it wouldn't thrill any man to know his wife was jetting around the world without him. I know there would be times when I would wish you'd be at home, and instead you'd be at the other side of the world. But that's you, Claire, that's your life, and I wouldn't want to make you change it. I'd like the reassurance of marriage, but with it or without it I reckon I'd always know I could trust you, even if we were apart for quite a while.'

'You could,' Claire agreed. She was silent for a moment, working out what to say, and how. She knew it was vitally important to them both that she should get this right, that she should be sure of what she said, and sure that she wouldn't make any offers she couldn't live up to without regrets. 'But it won't be forever, Jake. I won't always want to travel. I do love my job, but I love the thought of having a family, too. I won't want to travel as much as I do now when—if—I have children. I'm not sure I'd ever give up photo-journalism completely, but I do know that my work pattern would have to change, and change a lot.'

'You want that? You want children, you want to stay at home?'

'Oh, yes.' Then a sudden mist of apprehension swirled around her, and she added, uncertainly, 'Don't you?'

'Yes, definitely, though perhaps not straight away. You're young still, we could afford to wait a year or two, or even five. That would be time enough for you to establish yourself properly, to get all the wanderlust out of your system, wouldn't it?'

'It would,' Claire agreed. Her mind was working so fast that she was feeling dizzy. She so much wanted to believe that it would work. A part of her was bursting with joy, at the realisation that she had been offered the one thing she wanted more than anything else in the world. But at the same time she couldn't help feeling apprehensive. She had so nearly made a mistake with Philip; she had tried so hard to persuade herself that it wouldn't work with Jake. She didn't want to turn around and commit herself too quickly, before she was quite

ertain that they had both looked at the problems from
very angle.

'I think I could cope too,' she said slowly. 'If I wasn't
ravelling, there would be only half the number of separations. It wouldn't be easy for me either, holding the
ort alone while you travelled, but I think I could manage
.' She looked up at him, and gave a wry smile. 'You
eemed so footloose when I met you. A wanderer who
ked to travel alone. It'll take me a while to get used to
his new idea of you as a family man. But I know I could
rust you, darling. I've no doubt about that.'

Slowly, Jake's face relaxed into its familiar, and so
ovable, easy grin. 'Hold on, honey,' he said. 'I won't
e travelling forever, either.'

'You won't?'

'Hell, no. Not when we're married.'

'But I thought——'

He shook his head decisively. 'The work and my life-
tyle have fed each other, in a way. I was able to travel
ecause I hadn't any commitments back home, but at
he same time I always wanted to travel, because I wasn't
ure I'd be able to cope with the empty home-life I'd
ace otherwise. It's not something that all structural en-
ineers have to do. Several times I've been offered desk
obs. I had an offer only a few months ago of a partner-
hip in my company that would have meant much more
nanagement and less fieldwork. I turned it down at the
ime, but I'm pretty sure they'll make the offer again.
Next time, I reckon I'll take it.'

Claire stared at him. Then suddenly she began to
augh.

'So *I* wasn't sure it would work because *you* were
letermined to keep moving, and *you* weren't sure it
vould work because *I* was determined to keep moving!'

Jake joined in the laughter, throwing his head back and letting his amusement boom across the restaurant. When he sobered again, he said gently, 'And when it comes down to it, we'd both choose each other over the rest of the world.'

'Any time,' Claire said fervently. 'Mind you, I wouldn't want us to turn our backs completely on the rest of the world.'

'I can't see there's any danger of that,' Jake assured her. 'It's one of the compatible things about us that we both like to travel. Imagine how wonderful it will be when we travel together.'

Claire could imagine it, the expression on her face told him so. Jake watched her for a moment, then he went on, 'I've been looking over an assignment that would call for me to spend two weeks in Java. Maybe if we planned a honeymoon...'

'A working honeymoon? Oh, no! Even in Java, I'm not having you working on our honeymoon!'

'Heavens, no! I was thinking if we travelled over there a fortnight early, I took a couple of weeks off, and then we both stayed on while I did the assignment, that might suit us both.'

'Mmm. A honeymoon in Java...' Claire said dreamily. She had never been to the Far East, but she liked the idea, she liked it very much.

Perhaps she would be able to arrange an assignment for herself in Java, she began to think. Surely there would be a magazine somewhere which would welcome a travel piece? Even if there wasn't, she'd be able to take her camera with her and shoot some pictures. Maybe she could start to make a slow transition away from journalism, and towards more artistic travel photography.

'That would be in January,' Jake said. 'In five months' time. I don't want us to rush things this time. I know it's well over a year since we met, but we've seen so little of each other, it's not as if we've been together for a whole year. We need to get to know each other much better before we marry. But I want to make a commitment now, something that will help us both through all the separations.'

'A five-month engagement,' Claire echoed, savouring the thought. The idea of being engaged to Philip hadn't really made any impression on her, but she sensed that being engaged to Jake would be a very different matter, and not only because their intimate relationship would be such a world apart from hers and Philip's. On every level, it would be a time to come to know him as well as she possibly could. He would be her man, in every sense. And she really would feel like his woman, she thought to herself, even when they were a long distance apart.

'It sounds like a long time, I know,' Jake said, 'but I doubt if it will seem it. We have to plan how we'll schedule our work, and even where we'll live. I want you to come and meet my family very soon, and I hope I'll see some more of your parents. I want you to have a perfect wedding, with everything planned just right. I don't want us to wait too long—in a way I'd like to marry you tomorrow! But I think that's about the way we should plan to time it.'

'It sounds right,' Claire agreed.

'I know it won't always be easy. There will be times when we're apart, times when we both get lonely. I'm sure there will be times when we resent each other's work, and all that it does to keep us from each other.'

'True,' Claire agreed. 'But it would be worth working hard to hold on to what we have.'

'What we did have,' Jake gently corrected her. 'And what we will have again.'

That's only half right, Claire thought, as happiness slowly began to take root inside her. All the important things I have right now. There's more to learn about Jake, much more. I need to spend more time with him, he's right about that. But the love is there now, as it always has been, ever since that first strange meeting. All I need now is a chance to show it again.

She ached to reach across and touch him that very moment. But there was no need, because Jake himself was reaching across, to take her hand, and to bring it to his lips. His mouth just brushed the back of her hand, in a gesture that was formal and yet subtly erotic. And his hand kept holding hers, with his fingers softly tracing a pattern of desire across the sensitive skin of her palm and wrist, as his eyes met and held hers across the table.

A formal proposal, bouquets of flowers, a beautifully planned white wedding, and a honeymoon in Java. He had thought it all out, Claire realised, bemused. She had loved the steely side of Jake, the dangerous excitement of the stranger in cut-off jeans that she had first met, but there was a romantic streak in his nature too, and she was going to love that even more, she thought to herself now.

She smiled at the thoughts that were tumbling through her head. This was a man who matched her in every dimension. She might have to work hard to mesh her life with his, but it would be more than worth it, for in him she had found everything that she had ever wanted in a man, and more. She hadn't thought it was possible to ask for so much from life and get it all, but she had!

'All we need is the champagne,' she said teasingly.

'Oh, it's on its way. I asked the restaurant to chill a bottle for us. But there's something else we need, too.'

He reached in his pocket, and brought out a little box. 'I thought of letting you choose a ring, and then I thought, no, this is the right way to do it.'

Nestling in the box was the prettiest ring Claire had ever seen: a Victorian love-knot, sprinkled with tiny diamonds. 'Jake,' she whispered, 'it's beautiful.'

'Like you.' He said it in the happy knowledge that she believed him now, believed him totally. Carefully, he slipped the ring out of its mounting, spread her fingers, and slid it home. It fitted perfectly.

Claire gazed at the picture in front of her. Two hands entwined: one large and strong, tanned and unmistakably masculine; one neat and feminine—and marred, she saw, amused, by an inkstain that all her scrubbing hadn't completely rubbed away. And, on them, the ring that was itself entwined: a love-knot.

He had seen this too, she thought. He had chosen it with the deepest care, knowing the problems that would face them as well as the joys.

Two lovers linked and meshed together. Claire and Jake would be, sometimes. At other times they would find themselves a thousand miles apart. But still, somewhere in their hearts, they both knew they would always be entwined as closely as the knot on Claire's engagement ring.

Harlequin Presents®

Coming Next Month

#1327 A LOVE AFFAIR Lindsay Armstrong
Ashley returns to her father's farm after her husband's death. All she wants is to make a home for her daughters and get the farm running properly again. She certainly hadn't counted on the mocking, disturbing presence of Ross Reid.

#1328 IN SPITE OF THEMSELVES Elizabeth Barnes
Shy, reserved and conventional, Anne Chapin is nicknamed "Ice Princess." Yet she agrees to pose as mistress of prominent businessman Nicholas Thayer It wasn't part of the bargain but it leads to a wholly new bittersweet experience of unrequited love.

#1329 WEB OF DECEIT Amanda Browning
A rich man's mistress—or a loving daughter trying to shield her family? Eve knows which is her real self. For a moment she thinks Carl Ramsay does, too—then learns he's been taken in by the role she's being forced to play.

#1330 STORM FORCE Sara Craven
Maggie has enough problems—she really doesn't want anything to do with a macho TV hero involved in a tabloid sex scandal. But that is difficult when she finds Jay Delaney hiding out in her house....

#1331 A KISS BY CANDLELIGHT Joanna Mansell
Cathryn had somehow agreed to look after her boss's injured brother for two weeks. She's a secretary not a nursemaid. Sir Charles had warned her that Nicholas is a bad-tempered bully—not that he is also a very attractive man!

#1332 FORTUNE'S MISTRESS Susan Napier
Nick Fortune is angry enough at the apparent friendship between socialite Maggie and his sheltered daughter—what will he say when he finds it is Maggie's husband who's really involved with the girl? Nick doesn't know that Maggie's marriage is a sham, or that Maggie is attracted to Nick himself.

#1333 THE PRICE OF PASSION Elizabeth Oldfield
Gabrielle's disastrous love affair with Saul O'Connor had made her look for fulfillment elsewhere. Now with a chain of successful shops and a beautiful home, she is sure that she doesn't need Saul's love.

#1334 FIRE ISLAND Sally Wentworth
After her husband's death, Casey Grant concentrated on her career as director of an art and design agency. So when she falls for her client, Ivo Maine, on a business trip to Lanzarote, she is overwhelmed and confused about what she should do.